D0277914

Rhino What You Did Last Summer

Rhino What You Did Last Summer

ROSS O'CARROLL-KELLY
(as told to Paul Howard)

Illustrated by
ALAN CLARKE

PENGUIN
IRELAND

PENGUIN IRELAND

Published by the Penguin Group
Penguin Ireland, 25 St Stephen's Green, Dublin 2, Ireland (a division of Penguin Books Ltd)
Penguin Books Ltd, 80 Strand, London WC2R ORL, England
Penguin Group (USA) Inc., 375 Hudson Street, New York, New York 10014, USA
Penguin Group (Australia), 250 Camberwell Road, Camberwell, Victoria 3124, Australia
(a division of Pearson Australia Group Pty Ltd)
Penguin Group (Canada), 90 Eglinton Avenue East, Suite 700, Toronto, Ontario, Canada M4P 2Y3
(a division of Pearson Penguin Canada Inc.)
Penguin Books India Pvt Ltd, 11 Community Centre, Panchsheel Park, New Delhi - 110 017, India
Penguin Group (NZ), 67 Apollo Drive, Rosedale, North Shore 0632, New Zealand
(a division of Pearson New Zealand Ltd)
Penguin Books (South Africa) (Pty) Ltd, 24 Sturdee Avenue, Rosebank, Johannesburg 2196, South Africa

Penguin Books Ltd, Registered Offices: 80 Strand, London WC2R ORL, England

www.penguin.com

First published 2009

2

Copyright © Paul Howard, 2009
Illustrations copyright © Alan Clarke, 2009

Penguin Ireland thanks O'Brien Press for its agreement to Penguin Ireland
using the same design approach and typography, and the same artist,
as O'Brien Press used in the first four Ross O'Carroll-Kelly titles

The moral right of the author and illustrator has been asserted

All rights reserved
Without limiting the rights under copyright
reserved above, no part of this publication may be
reproduced, stored in or introduced into a retrieval system,
or transmitted, in any form or by any means (electronic, mechanical,
photocopying, recording or otherwise), without the prior
written permission of both the copyright owner and
the above publisher of this book

Set in Garamond MT 13.5/16 pt
Typeset by Palimpsest Book Production Limited, Grangemouth, Stirlingshire
Printed in Great Britain by Clays Ltd, St Ives plc

A CIP catalogue record for this book is available from the British Library

ISBN 978-1-844-88174-1

www.greenpenguin.co.uk

Penguin Books is committed to a sustainable future
for our business, our readers and our planet.
The book in your hands is made from paper
certified by the Forest Stewardship Council.

Contents

'We may see the small value God has for riches
by the people he gives them to.'
Alexander Pope

Prologue

The old man looks up at us, over the top of his reading glasses, and says the *cunillo* is wonderful.

Erika lifts her glass and goes, 'Happy New Year,' but I'm too in shock to return the toast. So her and the old man end up just clinking glasses.

'It will be,' he goes. 'It will be now.'

I look at *him*, then back at her. I don't see it. I don't see any resemblance at all. Or maybe I don't want to see it. It's one of those shocks that's, like, too big to take in all at once.

I stand up. Except I don't actually *remember* standing up? Let's just say I find myself suddenly standing up.

He turns to her and goes, 'Oh, here comes the waiter – have you decided what you're going to have?'

She's practically popping out of that black satin bustier, but of course I'm not allowed to even notice shit like that anymore.

I've got to get out of here. I stort walking. I hear *him* call me. I hear *her* call me as well. But I keep going.

I walk out of the restaurant, out of the hotel and out onto the street. It's snowing – coming down pretty heavy, in fact.

I get in the cor, turn the key – still in a daze – and point her in the direction of actual Barcelona.

I put my foot down and I'm suddenly tearing along all these narrow cliff roads in the pitch dork with the snow blinding me, not giving a fock – if I'm being honest – whether I even crash?

But then my phone suddenly beeps. It's, like, a text message from Sorcha, saying that she and Honor are thinking about me and that they're hoping that we beat Ireland A. She obviously knows fock-all about rugby, but it's still an amazing message to get and I kill my speed, suddenly remembering everything I have to live for, and realizing at that moment exactly where I'm headed.

What happened back there in the restaurant has made me realize that I need to be with my family. I need to see my own daughter and I need to find out if there's still a chance with Sorcha. I focked things up there like only I know how. But I need to know if there's still something there. Because it's with her and Honor that I actually belong.

I notice a set of lights in my rearview and somehow I *know* they belong to Erika.

Soon I arrive at the border crossing. The dude operating the barrier can't believe it's me. His eyes are out on practically stalks. 'I hear eet on the reddio,' he goes. 'It hees true? We score a try hagainst Island?'

I nod. 'We also kept them to less than a hundred points,' I go, which *is* the bigger achievement.

'A try hagainst Island!' he goes. 'You are hero to all of Handorra!'

He waves away my passport. No interest in even seeing it. I look in the mirror and watch Erika's lights approach.

'Dude,' I go, 'can you do me a favour? I'm trying to give this bird behind me the slip . . .'

He's there, 'Ha crezzy fan, yes?'

I'm like, 'Something like that. Can you make sure there's some kind of paperwork she's got to fill in? As in, a lot of it?'

'For you,' he goes, lifting the barrier for me, 'effery theeng hees poseeble.'

I put the foot down and off I go again, snaking through the Pyrenees, and I'm suddenly having one of my world-famous intellectual moments, thinking about how much your life can change in the space of an hour. It's like, there I was earlier tonight, being carried around the pitch shoulder-high, the hero of a – pretty much – country, which I've now left behind and will probably never see again. *And* it turns out that Erika's my sister.

My mind drifts back to a day, whatever, six, seven years ago, the day her old dear's divorce from Tim became final. Erika was majorly upset. I called around, supposedly to offer my sympathies, and we ended up going at it like two jailbirds on a conjugal visit.

I snap back to reality, realizing, very suddenly, that the border guard won't be able to hold her for long – not with her chorms. And not in that bustier.

I put the foot down again.

It takes, like, two and a half hours, but I finally reach the airport. It's, like, two o'clock in the morning when I pull up outside the main terminal building, throwing the rental cor in a set-down area, not even bothering my hole to return it, just leaving the keys in the basically ignition.

I realize that I don't even have any baggage. All my clobber's still back at the oportment.

I peg it in and check the departures board, my eyes going up and down what to me is just a mass of letters, waiting for two words to jump out at me: Los Angeles. There they are.

LA. The Windy City. Call it what you want – but that's where I'm headed.

I miss Honor so much that when I think about her, it feels like I'm having a hort attack. And, if I'm being honest, Sorcha too, even *if* she's with an auditor now.

The flight leaves at, like, 7.00 a.m. I order a first-class ticket using my old man's credit cord – the least he owes me in the circumstances.

There's, like, a major crowd hanging around the actual departure gate. As I get closer, I realize that it's the Ireland A team. They must be going out on a chorter.

Suddenly, roysh, they're all turned around, looking straight at me, all in their blazers and chinos. We're talking Keith Earls. We're talking Jeremy Staunton. We're talking Johnny Sexton. I'm expecting words like *traitor* to be suddenly bandied around like there's *no* actual tomorrow? But someone – might even be Roger Wilson – storts clapping, roysh, then one by one they all join in and before I know it the sea of Ireland A players has suddenly ported, and I'm being given a guard of honour through the departures gate.

It's actually just what I need.

But it's as I'm reaching the end of the line that I hear her voice. 'Ross!' she goes.

Of course, I should keep walking – I don't know *why* I don't? Maybe because I hear one or two wolf-whistles from the Ireland A goys. I turn around. She's obviously been crying, from the state of her boat.

She goes, 'Please don't go!'

I'm there, 'I need to get my head around this – time, space, blahdy blahdy blah.'

'Do you think *I'm* not confused?' she goes. 'Do you think *I'm* not angry? How can I ever trust my mum again?'

I go to turn around. 'I'm going to spend some time with my daughter and my – still – wife.'

'*I* could come with you,' she goes. 'We could get to know each other.'

I'm there, 'Maybe down the line. Right now, I need to get my head straight – see Sorcha, maybe find out if there's still . . .'

'A chance?'

'I was going to say a sniff. But yeah.'

4

She suddenly throws her orms around me, buries her head in my chest, then on go the waterworks. Out of the corner of my eye, I can see one or two of the Ireland A players looking at me, obviously thinking, whoa, rather you than me, Dude.

I rub her bare back and tell her she should be wearing more. She pulls away and looks at me, rivers of mascara running down her face, and says she left the restaurant in such a hurry, she forgot her coat.

I kiss her on the forehead and her hair smells of, I don't know, almonds and dandelions. I feel a sudden and familiar tightening in my trousers and, hating myself, I quickly turn away from her and tell her that I'd love to stay longer, but I've got, like, a plane to catch?

1. Right back where we started from

'How do you like them babies?' he goes, pointing at his shoes with a rolled-up copy of the *Wall Street Journal*. 'John Lobb custom brogues. Want to know what they cost?'

I actually *don't?*

'Four! Thousand! Dollars!' he goes anyway.

Of course, I just shrug, because it doesn't matter *how* good the Toms are – a man wearing a bluetooth earpiece is only five-eighths of a man.

Still, it's not up to me to tell him.

'Cillian!' Sorcha goes. 'We're supposed to be showing Ross around the house – *not* what you're wearing?'

This isn't, like, jealousy or anything, but I've never worked out what she sees in this tosspot.

I mention – being nice more than anything – that it's some pile of stones and straight away he has to mention that Beechwood Canyon is one of *the* most prestigious addresses *in* the Hollywood Hills.

It's only focking rented anyway.

'Madonna used to live, like, up the road?' Sorcha goes. '*And* Forest Whitaker. And who else, Pookie?'

Pookie? Jesus!

He's there, 'Aldous Huxley – *if* that name means anything to you, Ross,' pretty much *looking* to be decked?

They lead me out into this, like, huge entrance hallway. 'It's essentially a classic, 1930s-style Spanish villa,' *he* goes. 'Ten thousand square feet. Twelve bedrooms. Sixteen bathrooms.

Eight-car garage. Pool. Spa. Home theatre. *Four* bars. Three-hundred-and-sixty-degree views . . .'

I pull a face as if to say, you know – wouldn't exactly be *my* cup of tea?

Then they lead me into the kitchen, which Sorcha mentions is – oh my God! – the kitchen she's, like, *always* wanted?

The whole gaff is like something off *MTV Cribs*, in fairness to it.

She's there, 'It's got, like, a gourmet centre island,' which I can see for myself, 'with, like, three Sub-Zero refrigerators, an *actual* chef's Morice stove, a Fisher and Paykel double-drawer dishwasher *and* a built-in Nespresso . . .'

'It's a limited edition one as well,' *he* goes. 'You can't buy them in the shops,' and then, for no reason at all, he storts doing these, like, stretching exercises. This is a goy, bear in mind, who never played rugby.

'Oh my God,' Sorcha goes, 'I haven't even asked you about your flight.'

I'm like, 'Yeah, the flight was fine,' pulling up a high stool. 'Bit wrecked after it.'

'Have you decided yet what you're going to do for a carbon offset?'

It's amazing. I've known Sorcha for, like, ten years – been married to her for, what, three and a bit? – and she still knocks me sideways with questions like that.

'Because what you *can* do,' she goes, 'to pay off your emission debt, is set up a standing order with one of those companies that plant trees on your behalf. That way you can fly *and* drive with no, like, guilt at all.'

'I already do,' would be the wrong thing to say, so instead I just go, 'Cool,' cracking on to actually *give* a fock about, I suppose, world affairs.

She asks me if I fancy a coffee and I tell her I'd actually prefer to see Honor, if I could.

'Bad news,' *he* suddenly goes, 'we've just put her down.'

Sorcha's like, 'Cillian!' and he's there, 'Sorcha, if you wake her now, she'll be awake for the night. And I told you I've got that report to read on the high default rates on subprime and adjustable rate mortgages and their likely impact on the US economy.'

Adjustable rate mortgages? I'm thinking, he's *getting* decked – I don't give a fock how much Sorcha likes him.

But then *she* goes, 'Ross hasn't seen his daughter for, like, three months, Cillian. He's just flown for ten hours,' and then she turns around to me and she's like, 'Ross, come on . . .' and she leads me back out into the hall and up this big, winding staircase.

Honor's is the fourth bedroom on the right. I push the door, but when I catch, like, a glimpse of her curls in the light from the window, I end up just, like, filling up with tears and I have to actually turn away. All I want to do – I don't know why – is peg it back down the stairs and out of there. But Sorcha grabs me in, like, a clinch and whispers that it's okay, I suppose I'd have to say soothingly, in my ear. 'Take your time,' she goes, running her hand through my hair, so I take a few seconds to, like, compose myself, then I turn around and, with her orm around me, Sorcha sort of, like, slow-walks me over to the bed.

I get down on my knees and watch her tiny sleeping face. She's so beautiful. 'I can't believe how much she's changed,' I go, 'even in that time.'

Sorcha tells me that she still looks like me, which she doesn't. She's actually a ringer for Sorcha, but it's still, like, a really nice thing for her to say?

I stroke her little cheek and go, 'I've missed you so much,' and she actually opens her eyes for, like, two or three seconds, then closes them again.

I turn around to Sorcha and go, 'I better let her sleep,' and Sorcha's like, 'Why don't you come back in the morning? You can take her for the day?'

I ask her if she's sure and she's like, 'Ross, I feel – oh my God – *so* guilty for taking her away from you,' and I tell her not to be stupid, then I tell her – because I obviously didn't want to say it in front of *him* – that she looks well herself, as in *really* well, as in really well to the point of pretty much incredible?

She says it's possible to be practically vegan in LA and that she's been pretty much existing on mango slices and tempeh sausage patties. She says she also can't believe how much she underestimated the power of the blender.

I tell her I'm not just talking weight-wise. I'm there, 'You're, I don't know, *glowing*? The States has always suited you,' remembering how well she always looked when she came back from her J1er and how it always made me feel guilty for doing the dirt on her while she was away.

She smiles and says thank you. She smells of buttermilk moisturizer and in normal circumstances – you *know* me – I'd try to throw the lips on her there and then. But I don't, because, well, I think deep down I know that the reason she looks so amazing is that *I* haven't been in her life.

'Hey, what are you doing tonight?' she suddenly goes.

I'm there, 'I was just going to head back to the hotel – basically crash.'

She's like, 'Okay, you're *not*? I'm going to take you to, like, *the* best hot dog place in – oh my God – the actual world.'

See, she knows I'm a focker for the hot dogs.

'You haven't lived until you've tasted these,' she goes.

We head downstairs and she tells Cillian she's taking me to Pink's. And even though he tries to play it cool, roysh, you can tell he's *not* a happy bunny? 'I thought you were tired,' he goes to me, showing me his entire hand. It's like playing poker with your focking granny.

I'm there, 'I think I'm getting my actual second wind.'

'Well, I'll come as well,' he goes, but Sorcha's there, 'Er – and leave Honor on her own? Cillian, you said you had work to do. We'll only be, like, an hour. Two at the most,' and I make sure to give him a big shit-eating smile on the way out the door.

We're heading for, like, North La Brea, but Sorcha tells me I can switch off the SatNav because she, like, *knows* the way? I ask her what she thinks of the cor – we're talking a BMW 650 convertible – and she goes, 'How did you even rent this – you don't have, like, a licence?' and I laugh and tell her that I borrowed JP's.

She's there, 'Oh my God, you could get into *so* much trouble for that,' then she shakes her head, roysh, as if to say, same old Ross, he's never going to change – thank God.

The queue for hot dogs is up the focking street and around the corner, but it's good because it gives us, like, an hour to catch up. 'Like, *all* the celebrities come here?' Sorcha goes. 'I saw Famke Janssen here a few weeks ago and I'm pretty sure Mila Kunis. And my really, really good friend Elodine – Honor goes on, like, playdates with her daughter, Jagger? – she saw Brody Jenner ordering a pastrami reuben. It's like, *Oh! My God!*'

I laugh. 'Don't take this the wrong way,' I go, 'because I mean it as an actual compliment – you've become, like, so American. You just seem really at home here.'

She smiles, I suppose you'd say, warmly. 'The only thing I don't like about LA,' she goes, 'is that the water is – oh my God – *so* hard. Look, my hair's frizzy – and that's even *after* an hour with my GHD . . .'

I give her, like, a sympathetic look.

'That's why all of the stars are getting Evian filtered into their boilers. It said in *People* that Rhea Durham's doing it – even though she's denied it.'

I tell her I can't believe the size of the gaff they've ended up in. 'Are Pricewaterhouse actually paying for it?'

'No – it's, like, a weird one?' she goes. 'Bob Soto, who's, like, the head of the department that Cillian's been seconded to, his wife is, like, an attorney and it's one of her clients who owns it. They've gone on, like, a cruise for a year and they needed someone to just, like, house-sit? When we saw it, we were just like, Oh my God!'

I'm there, 'I'd say you were.'

'I can't believe you won't stay with us,' she goes. 'You've seen it, Ross – there's loads of room.'

I'm there, 'No, I'm Kool and the Gang in the Viceroy. Hey, did I tell you I'm in the exact same room where Christopher Moltisanti stayed in *The Sopranos*?'

'Oh my God,' she goes, 'that must be, like, *so* expensive.'

I'm there, 'Fock it – the old man's paying. The least he owes me when you think about it.'

It's at that point that I probably should mention Erika. But I don't – maybe I'm enjoying being around Sorcha too much. Instead, I ask her about work.

'Well, work-wise,' she goes, 'the last few months have been, like, a fact-finding mission for me? Even just walking around Melrose or Robertson, I've got – oh my God – *so* many ideas for the shop back home. Betsey Johnson's got, like, vertical TV screens playing actual catwalk footage? It's like, oh my God – why has no one in Ireland even *thought* about that? Except BTs, obviously.

'And I'm thinking of having, like, a seating area with huge pink couches – PVC, obviously, not leather. If people are relaxed, they *will* spend. Elodine told me that and she studied actual retail.

'And even just the way they talk to you in the shops, Ross. If they see you with, like, two or three items, they come over to you and go, "Do you want me to start a room for you?" And then they, like, compliment you? They're like, "Oh my God, that is *such* a good look for you!" I'm going to start saying *all* of those.'

Then she asks me what's been happening in *my* life. I'm there, 'Well, you know about the whole Andorra thing – a try against Ireland A, blahdy blahdy blah. Let's just say there's going to be a lot of teams all of a sudden interested in my services . . .'

Sorcha's phone beeps. Except it's not a phone – it's, like, a pink BlackBerry? I presume it's a text from Cillian – still bulling – but she reads it with, like, her mouth open, then tells me that members of the National Restaurant Association are furious with Kevin Federline for appearing in a commercial as a fast-food worker dreaming of becoming a rapper. They say it demeans low-wage restaurant workers.

Of course, I'm left just shaking my head.

'Oh,' she goes, 'it's this, like, celebrity alert service – Cillian got me a subscription for Christmas. You get, like, *all* the news and gossip, straight to your phone, as it happens. Even photographs. Oh my God, I *have* to show you the giraffe-print Escada halter that Jada Pinkett Smith wore to the New York Fashion Fête.'

Luckily, roysh, it doesn't come to that, because we're suddenly at the top of the queue. I order, like, a chilli cheese dog with, obviously, fries and I persuade Sorcha to have, like, a Patt Morrison Baja Veggie, even though she says she's trying to steer clear of guacamole.

We end up sitting in this little, I suppose, yord at the back of the place, at a little white plastic table, wolfing down what I would have to say is the most incredible hot dog I've ever tasted.

Sorcha mentions that she's going to buy Ayaan Hirsi Ali's autobiography again. 'I was only talking to Elodine the other night about her whole struggle?' she goes. 'And I thought, oh my God, I *have* to re-read it.'

I swat away a mosquito the size of a small bird, then I tell her it's great to see her. She smiles at me – like old times – and says it's great to see me, too.

The ugly munter – what is she, following me now?

She's all, 'What you're asking me, I think, is why do I write? And the answer to that is that I can't imagine *not* writing . . .'

I'm, like, shouting at the TV, going, 'You swamp donkey! You total focking mong!'

'I know this is going to sound, oh, impossibly celestial,' she's giving it, 'but sometimes it's as if my fingers are being directed – that I'm merely a cipher for this wonderful story that the universe has determined *must* be told.'

'*Karma Suits You*,' the dude interviewing her goes. 'Hey, what a crazy title – what's it about?'

'Well, it's the story of a fifty-something Irish woman who experiences a sexual reawakening – a re-blossoming, if you like – after going through the menopause. She abandons her old, rather repressed life *in* Ireland and comes to America, where she experiences this rebirth, which is where the idea of karma comes in. And of course she meets all these wonderful men – a fireman, obviously, a two-hundred-pound NBA star, even an elevator repairman – and has all these wonderfully erotic experiences, some of which she would have considered impossible without recourse to heavy pain medication . . .'

I'm, like, screaming now. 'You're a focking disgrace! You absolute focking manatee!'

'Of course, the full title,' the other interviewer – who's, like, a woman – goes, 'is *Karma Suits You – States of Ecstasy*. Because during the course of her year, she has – let's just say – *relations* with fifty men in fifty different states. And, controversially, fifty different positions. Can I just read out a line from one of my favourites, which is Alaska? This is the scene that ends with the kneeling lotus.

'*He said he was a whale fisherman. She looked at him askance, studying his leathery face, his commanding, callused hands, his entire bearing, straight as a longboat. Her resistance melted like the polar ice cap. Soon, he was exploring her Inside Passage and she was groaning like an age-worn sled dog.*'

The audience claps – they actually clap. 'You're a focking shambles!' I'm going.

Suddenly there's, like, a loud knock on the door, then it bursts open before I get a chance to even get out of the sack. There's all of a sudden a man stood at the foot of my bed – black, if the truth be told – and he's wearing, like, a uniform. At first, roysh, I think he's a cop, but then he says he's, like, hotel security.

'Sir,' he goes, 'we've had a complaint from one or two guests about a ruckus coming from this suite.'

'A ruckus?'

'A ruckus, Sir.'

I nod in the direction of the old Savalas. 'Well, can you actually blame me?'

He turns around, looks at the screen. '*Regis and Kelly*,' he goes. 'My wife never misses it. Though I gotta tell you, I *think* she preferred Kathie Lee . . .'

'I'm talking about *her*, the guest – focking so-called – they've got on . . .'

He sits on the end of the bed. 'She's kinda pretty,' he goes. 'She Irish?'

I'm like, 'Pretty? You've got to be shitting me – that's a double-bagger if ever I saw one.'

He's there, 'Got nice pins, too. What *you* got against this lady?'

'What I've got against her is that she *happens* to be my old dear.'

'Old what?'

'It's, like, our word for mother? And it's, like, how would you like to see *your* mother up on the wall there talking filth?'

'I wouldn't, I guess. But I gotta tell you, you gotta keep it down, my man. You in the Viceroy now – not the Y. You hearing me?'

I tell him I am.

'I'm Carl,' he goes.

A high-five in LA, I'm happy to say, is exactly the same as a high-five back home.

'No more ruckus – know what I'm saying?'

I'm there, 'Kool and the Gang, my friend. Kool *and* the Gang.'

Then he's suddenly gone.

My phone beeps – a text from, like, Sorcha: OMG ur mum is on live with regis n kelly! u must be omg SO proud.

'Because I think it's our duty,' the stupid hound's going, 'and I don't use that word lightly, *as* writers to challenge norms, be they sexual, be they . . . whatever.'

'Yeah,' this Kelly one's going, 'back in the, er, Emerald Isle . . .'

'The Old Sod,' Regis or whatever he's called goes.

'. . . you're considered something of an Irish Catherine Millet – would that be fair to say?'

'I think it would,' the old dear goes, 'insofar as we're both libertines. We both believe in free expression *in* a sexual context. *And* in all its forms, whether that's nihilism, sadomasochism, autoerotic asphyxiation . . .'

I can't actually listen to any more of this. I reach down, grab one of my Dubes off the floor and fock it straight at the TV. It bounces off, roysh, and I'm lying there thinking, it's a good job *I* don't wear John Lobb custom brogues, otherwise it would have probably cracked the . . .

The next thing, roysh – pretty unexpected, I have to say – the TV just, like, falls off the wall and there's what would have to be described as a loud explosion, we're talking sparks everywhere.

I'm like, 'Holy fock!'

I pick up the phone, dial zero for reception. I'm there, 'Listen, tell Carl not to bother his orse coming back up – everything's cool. By the way, I've pretty much broken the TV. Is that likely to show up on the Harry Hill?'

I was convinced that Sorcha was shitting me when I saw them first.

Stilettos for babies.

I asked her was it not, like, dangerous, but she said that girls eventually *have* to learn to wear designer heels and it's best if they stort young.

I *could* have pointed out that Chloe back home has been told she has to have both hips replaced, the result of a lifetime wearing designer heels, but it's, like, no – I'm actually over here to chill. So I said nothing while she put on Honor's little red patent pumps – '*so* like my *actual* Roger Viviers' – and warned me not to let her walk more than a few steps unassisted.

So we're sitting in, like, Bornes and Noble in Santa Monica – in the little Storbucks in there? – and it's nice, roysh, just the two of us, me and my daughter, spending some QT together, watching all the comings and goings.

Sorcha, I should mention, feels it's important for Honor to get a good grasp of conversational Spanish and Mandarin while she's still young. She said I wouldn't believe how important multi-ethnicity is over here. Every time someone passes our table, Honor's either like, '*Hola*,' or she's like, '*Ni hao*,' and the thing is, roysh, I haven't heard her say a word in actual English yet.

I'm there, trying to get her to say, 'Daddy,' going, 'Can you say, "Daddy"? "Daddy"! "Daddy"!'

'*Ni hao*,' she just goes. '*Ni hao ma*.'

She's also, by the way, trying desperately to get her hands on my grande triple shot *dulce de leche* mocha and I'm thinking, she's definitely my daughter. I end up giving her one or two little sips, thinking, you know, coffee can't be any worse for a baby than Toms that cut off the circulation in her feet.

So I'm sitting there, roysh, basically chilling, taking in the whole California experience, when all of a sudden there's a bird, we're talking one or two tables away – a ringer for Mandy Moore and that is *not* an exaggeration? – staring over, which is no big deal actually, because I *am* looking well at the moment and, as we all know, *every* bird is a sucker for a man with a baby.

'Oh my God!' she goes at the top of her voice. 'I *love* her!' which is always nice for a father to hear.

I'm there, 'Thanks. She's basically eighteen months old now – maybe a little bit more.'

It's only when she goes, 'She is such an inspiration to me,' that I realize that who she's *actually* talking about is Ayaan Hirsi Ali and the book I'm considering buying for Sorcha but am currently using as a coaster. 'Have you, like, read it?' she goes.

'Yeah,' I go, thinking on my feet as usual. 'Matter of fact,

I'm re-reading it? It's just I was talking to someone the other day about her whole, I suppose you'd have to say, struggle and I was thinking, Dude, you owe it to yourself to re-read it. And maybe re-read it again after that.'

She smiles at me. She's got teeth like Chiclets and she's interested in me – that much she's making pretty obvious. 'The bit where she's forcibly circumcised,' she goes, 'I was thinking, oh my God, if I could get my hands on those tribal elders . . .'

'Don't get me storted,' I go, then of course I haven't a clue what to say next – I don't know what the book's even about? – so I flip it over subtly and stort feeding her lines off the back cover.

'My own personal feeling,' I go, 'is that she has an open mind that has released itself from the old straitjacketed frame of reference of Right and Wrong. I mean, there's no doubt she is instinctively, deeply anti-authoritarian and – you'd have to say – unlikely to stick to straight ideological themes and shit? She will go on asking difficult questions. I could be wrong – that's just what I think.'

I thump the table then, just for effect.

No bird has ever looked at me the way she looks at me then – not even Sorcha on our wedding day. She wants me, and she wants me in a major way.

She goes, 'I know a guy who's hoping to turn her story into a Broadway musical. I would *so* love to play her.'

She sort of, like, indicates the chair beside me to ask if she can join me. I'm there, 'Yeah, coola boola,' because, like I told you, she's hot – and wearing half-nothing as well.

'I'm Sahara,' she goes, offering me her hand, the one that's *not* holding her frap?

I'm there, 'Sahara? What a beautiful name,' which it's not, of course – it's the name of a casino.

'It's actually Sarah?' she goes. 'But my agent thought it would help get me roles.'

I tell her I know a bird called Sophie who started spelling her name Seauphie as a way of, like, pissing off her old pair when they were getting divorced. It helps to get, like, a rapport going? Then I'm like, 'Hang on – did you say agent?'

'I'm an actress,' she goes.

I'm like, 'An actress?' showing an actual interest, which is something I'm going to stort doing more of. 'What are the chances! Well, without blowing my own trumpet here, I'm a pretty big deal myself back home.'

'Back home?' she goes. 'You mean you're not from California?'

I'm there, 'Er, my *accent*?'

She's like, 'You don't have an accent.'

'Are you shitting me?'

'No – where are you from?'

'I'm, like, Irish?'

'Oh my God, that is *so* random. I would never have known. So what are you, like, famous for in Ireland?'

'Well, not *just* Ireland, I could say. Have you ever heard of a certain game called rugby?'

'Rug . . .'

'Rugby?'

'I don't think so.'

I crack my hole laughing. 'Now I *know* you're shitting me.'

She has un-focking-believable Jakki Deggs, in fairness to her, smooth and tanned, and the way she's dangling her Havaiana on the end of her foot is doing it for me in a big-time way.

I'm there, 'Would it be rude of me to ask you for your number?'

She opens her mouth, only cracking on to be shocked. 'I'll

say this for you,' she goes, 'you're confident,' and I'm there, 'It *has* been said,' flirting my orse off majorly.

She's there, 'I bet it has. I only stopped by your table because I've just finished reading the same book,' playing the innocent, of course.

'You stopped by my table because you were attracted,' I go. 'You liked what you saw and you went for it – no one's judging you.'

She slaps me, sort of, like, playfully? You always know you're in when they do that. I'm there, 'So, what are doing Friday night?'

'What am I doing Friday night?' she goes, actually embarrassed. 'Oh my God, I can't believe I'm having this conversation. I'm having some of my girlfriends over. It's, like, my television debut? This thing I worked on . . . I don't know, do you want to come over?'

I'm there, 'Well, I've no other plans – plus I've broken the TV in my hotel room.'

I whip out my phone and she gives me her digits. She says it'll be me and, like, three girls there and I tell her I like those odds. She laughs. I put my hand on her knee, then she's suddenly serious again, fanning her face with her hand and saying *oh my God* over and over again, unable to believe her actual luck here.

But, like I said, think Mandy Moore.

I tell her I hoped she didn't get the wrong idea when she saw me with my daughter. 'Don't worry,' I go, 'I'm happily separated – on the way to being divorced. Yeah, *she's* with, like, a complete tosser now – he's, like, an auditor.'

Of course, I end up nearly falling off the chair when she turns around and goes, 'What daughter?'

I look beside me. My coffee has gone and, more importantly, so has Honor and I pretty much crap my board shorts. It's like, No! No! No!

The next thing, roysh, I'm literally running around the shop, calling her name at, like, the top of my voice, while at the same time kacking it – and who can blame me? I check, like, Crafts and Hobbies, Architecture, even Humanities and she's, like, nowhere to be seen.

On the outside, I'm trying to stay calm. I tell Sahara that she couldn't have gone far – she isn't walking that long. *And* she's in, like, high heels. But then I remember that she's had a coffee – the guts of a triple espresso – and I realize that she could be anywhere.

Then of course the guilt storts to kick in. I'm thinking about all the people down through the years who told me that this pretty face would eventually be my undoing and how they'd love to see me now, frantically running around Recommended, Judaism and Judaica and – this'll give you a laugh – Parenting, looking for my actual daughter, who wandered off while I was busy playing Mr Lover Lover.

Sahara, in fairness to her, keeps her head. She asks me for, like, a description, then says she'll tell security to lock down the store. 'If she's in here,' she goes, 'we'll find her – you go check outside.'

Outside? I hadn't even thought! I literally burst through the doors, out onto Third Street, and stort pegging it up the promenade like an actual lunatic. Every baby I see, I run, like, straight up to them, going, 'Honor!' and of course when it's not her, the parents are looking at me as if to say, 'Er, *weirdo*?'

It must be, like, half-a-mile up the promenade that I decide to give up, thinking, there's no way she could have got this actual far. That's when I notice this, like, ruck of people gathered around this crowd of buskers playing, like, salsa music. It's actually out of the corner of my eye that I *think* I spot a mop of blonde curls somewhere in the middle and I'm literally throwing people out of the way to get in there.

It's her! She's standing in front of the band, in her little red shoes, dancing away. And everyone's laughing and clapping, like they think she's part of the act?

'That's my daughter!' I go. 'That's my actual daughter!' and I sweep her up in my orms.

'Hey, Man, I was enjoying that,' someone shouts and then someone else goes, 'Asshole,' but I don't give a fock now that I've got her back, unhormed as well, although her body *is* sort of, like, twitching in my orms and she keeps, I don't know, clenching and unclenching her teeth.

'Is she okay?' this bird asks me. She's not that unlike Trista Rehn. 'Her eyes look kind of spacey.'

'Yeah, she's had a coffee,' I go, then she looks at me like I'm some kind of, I don't know, monster.

I carry her back up the street, promising to buy her all sorts of shit and grateful, I suppose, that she doesn't have the words yet to tell Sorcha what happened – certainly not in any language that her mother could understand.

Sahara – Sarah, whatever – is waiting for me at the door of Bornes and Noble. 'You found her!' she goes and then, 'Oh my God, she's *so* beautiful!'

I'm shaking my head going, 'If anything ever happened to her, I'd . . . well, I don't know what I'd do.'

She smiles, then leans forward and gives me the most unbelievable kiss on the lips, to the point where I'm suddenly feeling a bit spacey myself. 'You are *such* a sweet guy,' she goes. Then she hands me, like, a bag. 'I hope you don't mind – I bought that book *for* you?'

Sorcha asks me how Honor was yesterday and I tell her fine.

That's one of the good things about being a lady's man my entire life – I can lie without even thinking about it?

'It's just that it took me – oh my God – hours to get her to sleep last night,' she goes.

I pull a face like I'm trying to come up with, I don't know, the answer to a really hord crossword question? Then I shake my head. 'I don't know what that could have been.'

I'm just there, bouncing Honor up and down on my knee, going, 'I think it was just the excitement of seeing your Daddy again, wasn't it?'

'*Xing qi yi . . .*'

'Can you say, "Daddy"?'

'*Xing qi er, xing qi san . . .*'

Sorcha suddenly gets a text. She says that – oh my God – actress Julia Roberts and husband filmmaker Danny Moder are going to have a little brother or sister for Hazel and Phin. I just shrug. Then she goes, 'Oh my God, there's one about your mum, too,' and I have to admit, roysh, she suddenly has my attention. 'Oprah was spotted reading a copy of her book in The Rosebud in Chicago. Oh! My God! That is *such* a huge deal, Ross.'

I crack on not to be impressed. 'It's, like, who even *is* Oprah – I'm talking in the big scheme of things?'

She laughs and says that an endorsement from Oprah can turn a book into a million-seller overnight.

I shrug my shoulders. I'm like, 'The thing I don't under-stand is when did she even write it? She's only been in the States, like, a fortnight.'

'She wrote it when she was in, like, her twenties.'

'It's more of her usual porn.'

'It's *so* not, Ross. In fact, I was the one who told her to send it to an American publisher.'

'You?'

'About two years ago. I was the first one she ever let read it.'

She always was a crawler when it came to my old dear.

'She has this amazing line about Florida. *He exploded inside her like a first-phase rocket . . .*'

I suddenly cover Honor's ears. I'm there, 'Too much information, Sorcha! Too much information!'

She laughs, then takes Honor from me. She says that Cillian's late, meaning late home from work. I'm thinking that maybe now is the time to tell her about Erika. We're relaxing beside the pool with a couple of appletinis and I feel like I could say anything to her at this moment.

But I don't.

Instead, I end up talking about *him*. 'I think he feels threatened by me,' I go.

She's there, 'Cillian? Cillian has no reason to feel threatened by you,' except she says it a little bit *too* defensively?

I'm like, 'Some would disagree. What was all that shit the other night about his shoes? John focking Lobb.'

'Oh my God,' she goes, 'there's nothing wrong with wanting to look your best, Ross.'

'But he's an accountant.'

'Don't give me that – he happens to be a senior adviser in international risk assessment.'

'*Whatever!* It's not just the shoes anyway. It's the gaff – he thought he was Puffy showing me around his crib. All he was short of saying was, "This is where the magic happens!" which, I reckon, would have been bullshit anyway.'

She looks at me, suddenly embarrassed, and I immediately know it's a touchy subject. 'What do you mean by that?' she goes.

I'm there, 'Well, I couldn't help but notice *Prison Break*, Season One, on the bedside locker. Boxsets in the bedroom are a definite sign of somebody who's not getting any.'

'That's none of your business,' she goes, pointing at me, which she only ever does when I've hit the nail on the head. 'You've no right to even talk to me about that side of my life. We're both free agents, can I just remind you? We've both moved on.'

Now it's my turn to laugh. I think she's just made it obvious that she still misses me in at least one deportment. 'All I'm saying,' I go, 'is that Cillian shouldn't feel under pressure with me here. He shouldn't feel like he has to compete with me.'

'Oh, believe me,' she goes, 'he doesn't.'

The next thing we hear, roysh, is a cor pulling up outside, except it's obviously not the focking Prius Nerdster that Cillian drove to work this morning – you can tell from the sound of the engine. We walk around to the front of the gaff and I end up actually laughing out loud when I see him – this dude who's supposedly *not* threatened by me? – getting out of a brand new, red Murciélago.

He's still wearing his Magee suit, bear in mind – focking D'Arcy's crowd.

Sorcha's jaw is practically on the ground and not in a good way. She's like, 'Cillian, where did you get this?'

He's there, 'I bought it.'

It's an unbelievable cor, in fairness – totally focking wasted on him. We're talking six-point-two litre engine, we're talking four-wheel drive, we're talking six-speed sequential automatic transmission. We're also talking three hundred Ks and possibly more. She goes, 'How much did you pay for this?'

He immediately looks at me. I pull a face that says, basically, rather you than me, mate, listening to that.

'Does it matter?' he goes. 'I got a loan.'

'A loan?'

He's there, 'Yeah. I'm earning unbelievable money, remember,' which is an attempted dig at me – except I've never been interested in earning money, only spending it.

'More to the point,' Sorcha goes, 'how fuel-efficient is it?'

I just, like, snigger, kiss Honor goodbye, then leave them to it.

'This particular table,' he goes, 'has been meticulously engineered *and* crafted. Solid oak construction. One-inch diamond-honed slate. These pockets – genuine leather, hand-tooled.'

I run my hand across the felt.

'Heirloom quality, Man. You play?'

I shrug. 'It was pretty much *all* I did in college,' I go. 'But it's actually a present for my son?'

'Well,' he goes, 'not only will your son enjoy it, so will his son, and his son after that. Don't let anybody tell you any different – pool tables are a very sophisticated piece of equipment. There's no MDF in this thing. You hear what I'm saying? Solid! Oak! That's why you got to pay that little bit more . . .'

'I don't care,' I go. 'It's not even me paying.'

My phone suddenly rings. It's like, speak of the devil. 'What do *you* want?' I go.

He's like, 'Where are you, Kicker?'

I'm there, 'Los Angeles – what's it to you?'

'Oh,' he goes. 'Well, I'm still in Andorra. It's just that, well, you left in a bit of a hurry.'

'Is there any chance you could stop babbling for five seconds?' I go. 'Is your credit cord still good – the one with the 1982 Triple Crown-winning team on it?'

'Actually, no,' he goes. 'I've just this minute discovered it's been stolen.'

I'm there, 'Well, *actually* it hasn't? *I* took it. So don't cancel it. You're about to become the proud owner of a state-of-the-ort pool table,' and I tip the nod to the shop dude, who immediately storts filling in the shipping documents, happy in his pants.

At the top of my voice, I'm like, 'I'm going to take the jukebox as well – the big Wurlitzer jobby,' and, then into the phone, I go, 'Seven focking grand – I presume you're good for it.'

Of course, he doesn't even *give* a shit. 'I *hope* it's vinyl,' he goes. 'Oh, even the mention of the word Wurlitzer brings me back, Ross, back to the old days. The Rainbow what's-it on O'Connell Street. "There's No Other Like My Baby". That was our song – Helen and I . . .'

Helen as in Erika's old dear.

I'm there, 'I don't actually *give* a fock? I bought, like, a jacuzzi an hour ago – are you not even curious as to why?'

'Well, I expect you felt your *old dad* owed you a present after the heroics at the Camp d'Esports del M.I. Consell General . . .'

'No, that's *not* it. Do you remember when I was kid, the bomb shelter we found at the bottom of the gorden?'

'Oh, yes – chap we bought the house from was absolutely convinced that Truman was going to drop the big one on China, unleashing hell and what-not.'

'Whatever. Do you remember saying to me we were going to turn it into a boys' room and then never actually doing it?'

'Well,' he goes, 'if I said it, I'm sure it would have been in the context of – wouldn't it be wonderful if . . .'

'Oh, but you were too busy with work, weren't you? Doing all the dodgy shit they eventually put you away for. So now *I'm* turning it into a boys' room – for me and *my* son.'

'What a wonderful idea,' he goes.

It's, like, impossible to hurt this focker. I try to come in from a different angle. 'By the way, when are you going to do something about that scabrous animal?'

'Your mother?' he goes. Isn't it funny how he immediately knows? 'Yes, I hear she's making something of a splash, inverted commas, stateside.'

'She was on TV yesterday, making a holy focking show of me.'

'Well, this is the book she wrote during her famous Paris years. She was only in her twenties, Ross. They say it's her *magnum opus* – pardon the French.'

I'm there, 'Why are you defending her? You're supposed to be getting divorced. Why can't you, like, hate each other?'

'Hate each other?'

'Yeah, like *normal* parents?'

'We were married for thirty years,' he goes, like *that's* any kind of excuse. 'Your mother and I will always be friends. We care about each other very much.'

'Well, I just think that's focked up, that's all.'

He doesn't even respond to that, just goes, 'Erika's gone back to Ireland . . .'

I'm there, 'Er, did I *ask* you about Erika?'

'I think after the initial euphoria, the anger's starting to kick in. Helen called me today – seems that Erika said some hurtful things to her.'

'I said, I don't remember asking about her,' and then I just hang up.

'I can't believe you're actually shopping with me,' Sorcha goes. She has to shout it over a seriously loud disco version of 'Can You Feel The Love Tonight?', which means we're obviously in Abercrombie. 'You used to hate shopping.'

I'm there, 'If you must know, I was shopping all yesterday

afternoon. I picked up, like, a jukebox, pool table, a few other bits and pieces for Ro.'

She looks at me like, well, like she did the night she first took advantage of me when I'd a few beers on board in the Wez. 'You are *so* a good father,' she goes. 'Anyone who says you're not is, like – oh my God – *so* wrong . . .'

Having said that, if she finds out I let Honor wander around Santa Monica on her Tobler for half an hour, she'll redecorate this shop with my focking intestines.

'I know,' I go. 'I think it's very much a case of, you know, give a dog a bad name . . .'

My focking eardrums are bursting in here.

A changing room finally comes free. I automatically follow Sorcha in and the funny thing is that neither of us actually considers it weird – as in, her stripping down to basically her bra and knickers in front of me?

The bird in charge of the changing rooms does, though – she knocks on the door and goes, 'It's only *one* person per changing room?' and I end up just going, 'Yeah – *what*ever!' to which there's *no* comeback, of course.

Sorcha's, like, examining her orse in the mirror. 'Do you think these jeans make my legs look thinner than my Citizens of Humanity ones?' she goes.

It's one of those questions where she already *knows* the answer she wants? So I make what I have to admit is a guess, 'Yes.'

'What about my Sevens?' she goes. 'Are *they* more slimming?'

I go, 'No,' solely on the basis that last time I said yes. It's like Junior Cert. foundation maths all over again.

She considers my answers while striking, I suppose, different poses in the mirror – one hand on her hip, one foot in front of the other, then pouting, whatever the fock difference that makes – and finally decides that she doesn't want them. So they come off again.

'You don't mind?' I go. 'As in, me staring at you pretty much naked?'

She's like, 'I *have* underwear on, Ross? And anyway, it's nothing you haven't seen before, right?'

She looks unbelievable. A Peter Pan's always suited her.

I'm there, 'I wonder would Cillian see it like that.'

She pulls her sea blue Tart Grace dress over her head and goes, 'Cillian would be fine with it. I'm sorry about the other night, by the way.'

I'm there, 'Is he keeping it? As in, the Lamborghini?'

'Well, he's bought it now. Or signed the finance papers. I think he's just very stressed with work at the moment.'

'I'm saying nothing,' I go. 'But I still think it's me.'

She laughs. 'Oh my God, Ross, he *knows* that you and I are more like Best Friends Forever these days?' and I'm thinking, yeah, you just keep telling yourself that lie, girl.

She steps into her Uggs, fixes her hair, then puts her sunglasses back on her head, and I open the changing-room door. The bird outside is bulling. She's a last word freak as well. 'Only *one* customer per changing room?' she goes, pointing at a sign on the wall.

You actually *should* have seen her face when I pretended to do up my fly.

On the way out of the shop, out of the corner of her mouth, Sorcha's going, 'I can't *actually* believe you did that!' but she's also smiling, as if to say, I can't actually control this dude – might as well just sit back and enjoy the show.

Back in the cor, she checks her texts and says that Lindsay Lohan was spotted dancing with Blink-182 drummer Travis Barker at a West Hollywood party two days after having her appendix out!

'My kind of bird,' I go.

'And Angelina has dropped the broadest hint yet that she might like to work with Billy Bob Thornton again one day . . .'

To which there's no real answer.

I tell her I'm storving. I'd eat the orse out of a roadkill raccoon. She says okay, we'll collect Honor from crèche, then she's going to bring me – her treat – to Ketchup, as in Ketchup from *The Hills*? As in, the place where Lauren and Heidi ran into each other for the first time after the big fight? And Spencer sent over a drink for Lauren and Jason, being – oh my God – *such* a wanker?

I have to say, Spencer's always been my kind of goy.

Ketchup turns out to be a pretty amazing spot. I order a pepper-seared Kobe with fries, Sorcha has a twenty-first-century cobb without the chicken, the bacon or the blue cheese – a grassbox, in other words – and Honor has a plate of sweet potato tater tots, which I'm pretty taken aback to see her eating with chopsticks – as in, her own personal set?

I can't even eat with chopsticks.

'I can't believe you have her eating with those things,' I go and Sorcha ends up nearly biting my head off. She tells me I don't live here, so I have no idea how important the whole diversity thing is. She goes. 'Poet, one of Honor's playdates, is actually part Asian-American, Ross.'

I'd forgotten how sexy she can be when she loses it. But I'm also thinking how *nice* this actually is? As in, the three of us sitting here, back together as, like, a family again.

I'm there, 'How would you feel if I told you I had a date tomorrow night?'

She looks all of a sudden serious. 'Oh,' she goes. 'I mean, that was quick. Can I ask who?'

'You're not jealous, are you?'

'No, it's just – you only arrived, what, three days ago.'

'I've always been a fast mover – *you* know that. And if you must know, she's an actress.'

'An actress? Oh my God, what's she been in?'

She's bulling – as in, seriously bulling.

'Well, it's early days yet. Obviously, we want to keep things below the rador for now.'

Honor all of a sudden storts crying, for no actual reason at all. Some people would say that's women for you. She's not only crying, roysh, she's pretty much screaming the roof off, to the point where Sorcha has to take her out of her baby chair and sort of, like, bounce her on her knee.

'Okay,' she goes, 'just answer me this, is it Jessica Stroup?'

'I can tell you it's definitely not Jessica Stroup.'

'Torrey DeVitto?'

'No, it's not Torrey DeVitto.'

'Hilarie Burton?'

'Whoa, enough with the guessing already!'

'I'm sorry,' she goes. 'But if it'd been any of those, I *would* have been jealous . . . Come on, Honor, what's wrong?'

She offers her everything from her bottle to her Dora the Explorer doll to a spicy tuna roll, but there's no calming her.

'You're saying you're *not* jealous?' I go.

She shrugs. 'You're a free agent,' she goes, then she stares into space, obviously surprised at how badly it's affecting her.

She stands up very suddenly and says she has to go to the restroom – and she actually uses that word. 'See if you can do anything with her,' she goes, plonking this bundle of basically noise in my lap. 'You know, she's been so irritable the last couple of days, which isn't like her at all.'

That gets me suddenly thinking. I follow Honor's line of vision and realize that, yeah, she's staring straight at my Americano. All she basically wants is a sip of my coffee. So when Sorcha hits the jacks, I check that no one's looking, then I hold the mug up to her lips. She immediately stops crying. She has, like, three or four sips – five at the very most – and she's suddenly happy like you wouldn't believe.

'Oh my God!' Sorcha goes, suddenly back from the can. 'What did you do?'

I'm there, 'I don't know. Maybe I've just got, like, a way with her.'

She's like, 'You certainly do. I am, like, *so* impressed. So what do you want to do – do you want to hit one or two more shops in the afternoon?'

I'm there, 'Hey, I'm easy like a Sunday morning.'

'I am *so* excited about my plans for the shop,' she goes. 'Oh my God, I'm going to blow Coast and Reiss out of the water with the dresses I'm going to be bringing in. We're talking Literature. We're talking Bailey. We're talking KLS. We're talking Cash Lords. And a simple question – why is no one in Ireland doing Antik and Taverniti jeans?'

On the spur of the moment – and this is totally unrehearsed – I decide that that's my cue to bring up, like, the whole Erika situation? It's only a matter of time before she rings her anyway.

'Speaking of antics,' I go, 'the major news back home involves Erika.'

'Erika?'

'Exactly.'

'As in, my best friend Erika?'

She definitely thinks I'm going to tell her I was, like, with her – as in, *with* with? – so this might even turn out to be a bit of a relief to her. 'Before you say it, it's not what you think,' I go. 'No, the thing is, it turns out – now *how* random is this? – that she's kind of, well, my sister . . .'

'Your sister?'

'Well, half-sister really. She found out that that dude Tim was never her old man . . .'

'Hang on, Ross. I can't take this in. Erika . . . is your sister?'

'Yeah, her old dear came clean. Told her that her old man was a goy she had, like, a fling with in the seventies, eighties, whatever . . .'

'Er, I know that, Ross? I talked to her at Christmas?'

'Well, the goy she had the fling with turns out to be my old man . . .'

'Oh! My God!'

'Exactly – poor focking girl. How would you feel finding that out?'

Sorcha suddenly bursts into tears. 'Drive us home,' she goes without even looking at me. 'Now.'

'I thought you'd love the story,' I make the mistake of going. 'Especially with all those soaps you watch . . .'

She totally flips at that.

'She was, like, my Best *Best* Friend!' she practically screams at me.

I'm there, 'I dare say she still will be.'

'How *could* you, Ross?'

'What do you mean, how could *I*?'

'How could you do it?'

There's, like, silence in the restaurant. First Spencer and Heidi, now me and Sorcha – the drama never focking ends in this place.

I'm there, 'Er, this is one of those things that *isn't* my actual fault?'

'And you kept it to yourself this long?'

'Whoa,' I go, 'I only found out myself, like, four days ago.'

'Why didn't you say something the night you arrived?'

'Because I knew I had to get the timing right. And you *were* pretty keen for me to try those hot dogs. Which I thought were amazing, I don't know if I mentioned.'

Sorcha's shouting is drawing quite a lot of attention our way now. 'I never want to see you again,' she goes, standing up and pretty much snatching Honor out of my orms.

'Fair enough,' I go. 'Here, I'll give you a lift home.'

She's like, 'Actually, don't bother, Ross. We'll get a cab,' and then, just before she storms off, she takes one last look at me, narrows her eyes and goes, 'And whoever it is you're meeting tomorrow, she's welcome to you!'

Then she's suddenly gone, leaving me sitting there, picking my way through what's left of her salad, looking for something edible and at the same time thinking, that could have gone a *hell* of a lot worse.

I've spent, like, an hour walking up and down the beachfront in Santa Monica and I can honestly say I've seen more meat on a focking Barbie doll.

Los Angeles is one of those towns that could give even me a complex – that is, *if* I hadn't kept myself in such unbelievable shape.

This isn't me being big-headed, but I *am* looking the port, it has to be said, with the sunnies and the old pink apple crumble, which shows off my pecs really well.

A bird goes by me on rollerblades and ends up nearly snotting herself while checking me out. I end up just going, 'Drink it up, Baby – it's *full* of goodness,' though it's not in a sleazy way, because she actually loves it.

I sit down on a bench for a rest because the heat over here would actually wear you out. I whip out the Wolfe and dial the number. He answers on, like, the third ring.

I'm like, 'Christian, my man!'

'Ah, Ross,' he goes, obviously really delighted to hear from me. 'How the hell are you?'

I'm there, 'Not bad, Young Skywalker,' which he loves, of course. 'Although the question should be, *where* am I? Because I just so happen to be in a little town that goes by the name of . . . *Los* Angeles?'

'No way!' he goes.

I'm there, 'Yes way! You better believe it, Dude! It's happened! Just fancied a couple of weeks away — see a bit of Honor, possibly even Sorcha . . .'

'Oh, so you're staying in the mansion?'

'Not exactly. I'm in, like, a hotel. To be fair to her, Sorcha offered? But I don't want to cause trouble between her and that tosspot of hers.'

He's there, 'Yeah, *we* stayed with them. Cillian's an alright guy, Ross.'

'But he went to, like, Oatlands.'

'I know — but even so.'

I just laugh. 'Maybe. Whatever. I'm putting him under serious pressure, though. He's bought a Lamborghini.'

'A Lamborghini? Not the kind of thing you'd expect from an accountant, is it?'

'Obvious why, though, isn't it? His girlfriend's got the love of her life back sniffing around her. He's feeling threatened. Thinks he's got to prove his manhood.'

A bird walks by in literally just a bikini — a ringer for Hayden Panettiere. She has a good look — gagging for me.

'Hey, I read what happened in Andorra,' Christian goes. 'A try against Ireland A? That must have been . . .'

'Pandemonium — that's being honest.'

'Wow.'

'It was literally the closest thing to, like, Beatlemania that

I'll ever know. They were, like, carrying me around the pitch, pretty much shoulder-high, after the final whistle.'

'Really?'

'Big-time. It'll definitely go down in history as one of those moments – what were you doing the day when blahdy blah? Like the day – what was his name? – something Kennedy was shot?'

'Did it feel weird, though? You know, conspiring against your own country?'

'Well, we were ninety-something points down at the time. I don't think Michael Bradley's going to get the road for it. Oh, by the way – *I* did?'

'What?'

'Yeah, I got sacked.'

'Why?'

'Why do you think? Trying to dip the wick where it shouldn't have been dipped. In other words, the boss's wife. Still, you live and learn. Or at least that's the general idea. So what are *you* up to – do you fancy a boozy lunch?'

'What?'

'A boozy lunch. I'm in Santa Monica. I'll tell you what, you'd have some pole on you walking around over here, wouldn't you?'

He goes, 'Ross, we're in Marin County.'

I'm there, 'Oh. What would that cost you in a cab?'

'It's, like, a five-hour drive?'

'Whoa,' I go. 'It's a massive place, isn't it?' meaning the States. 'And obviously I can't just leave Lauren . . .'

'Oh, I forgot – she's about to drop, isn't she?'

'Yeah – and she's finding the last couple of weeks pretty tough-going.'

'It's going to be some year for you,' I go. 'Baby. Then work-wise obviously . . .'

I don't know if I mentioned that he's the project manager for the new *Star Wars*-themed casino in Las Vegas.

'Yeah, Mr Lucas loved my idea to style the helipad on the landing bay in the New Death Star. And to have, like, stormtroopers and royal guards escort the highrollers to the tables . . .'

I'm there, 'Oh, it's *Mr* focking Lucas, is it?'

It's great to hear my best friend in the actual world so excited about something.

'It's only six months to go, though. And there's, like, *so* much to do.'

'I'll tell you what,' I go, 'you stay where you are. *I'll* drive up to *you* – maybe next weekend . . .'

He's there, 'Er, cool.'

'Tell you everything that's happening. I haven't lost it, just in case you're wondering. I've got a sort of date tonight with an actress. Called – of all things – Sahara. She's invited me over to watch her TV debut with her and her mates. Planning to have my sweaty way with her, I don't need to tell you. The Rossmeister will never change, that much is guaranteed.'

In the background, I can suddenly hear Lauren asking him who's on the phone. He puts his hand over the mouthpiece, but I can still hear him go, 'It's Ross. He's *in* California. He wants to come up here . . .'

I don't hear what *she* says. Lauren, it has to be said, has always been very fond of me. 'Here, put me onto her,' I go. 'I'll tell her some of the shit I've been up to since I got here.'

Christian's like, 'She's, em, just going to have a lie-down,' and I'm there, 'Oh, cool – well, I'll see her next weekend, won't I? Say, Saturday?'

Who knocked Katherine Heigl into shape, Nia wants to know – like, she *has* to know? Corey says it was Harley Pasternak

– the man is, like, a God? Then Sahara says the Five Factor Diet is supposed to be *so* amazing.

Me, I'm sitting here like Jack focking Nicholson in the *Witches of Eastwick*, wrapping the old lips around a passion-fruit daiquiri, thinking even my critics back home would have to admit, on the basis of this, that my away form is every bit as incredible as my home form.

I'm here, what, less than a week? Fock knows what that is in hours, but here I am, in an unbelievable aportment on La Cienega Boulevard, wedged between Sahara, who wants me bad, and Corey, who's a banger for Odette Yustman, while Nia – if I *had* to compare her to someone, I'd have say Holly Madison – keeps giving me the old deep meaningfuls on the down-low, obviously thinking, I'll finish anything *they* don't.

And we're watching *Grey's Anatomy*, waiting to see Sahara's big TV debut, while milling our way through a table of food.

Corey says the hummus is – oh my God – *so* amazing and Sahara says she *wants* to put more wholegrain crackers out, but she's scared of, like, missing it?

'Is it going to be soon?' I go, getting a bit bored to be honest, and she's like, 'Yeah, it's coming up in, like, two minutes.'

I'm wondering is she going to be, like, a nurse. A corpse *would* be a bit of a let-down, it has to be said, though I suppose you've *got* to think in terms of what this could, like, lead to? I mean, I'm looking at her Wolfe Tone there on the table, thinking, *imagine* the focking numbers she's already got in there. The second she hits the shitter later, I'm going through it looking for Ellen Pompeo and Chyler Leigh. *And* Heigl, obviously.

Nia is giving me loads, by the way. She's all, 'So, Eye R Lind! That must be like, Oh! *My* God!'

'You'd be surprised,' I go. 'The circles *I* move in are pretty cool – pretty much the same as here, actually. The rest of the country's basically backward.'

From her reaction, I can tell she's pretty taken aback by my, I suppose, honesty. She thinks about what I've said for a few seconds, then suddenly smiles again and goes, 'So what do you think of WeHo girls?'

Of course I end up giving her a line that'd be, like, a trademark of mine back home? I'm there, 'I know what I like – and I *like* what I see,' which goes down unbelievably well.

'I still can't believe you're *all* actresses,' I go. Corey laughs at that, then tells me that *everyone* in this town is, like, an actor, actress – whatever! 'Not all of us have got major credits,' she goes, looking, you'd have to say, pretty proud of Sahara.

I'd say they definitely *would* if I put it to them?

All of a sudden, Sahara's shushing us, going, 'Here it comes! Here it comes!' and at first, I think it has to be a mistake, roysh, because it's not *Grey's Anatomy* anymore? It's, like, a commercial break and we're suddenly sitting there watching an ad for what turns out to be – and this is going to sound disgusting – a contraceptive coil.

I'm like, 'What the fock is this?'

It's like, 'Introducing Progestin-Plus – the new, no fuss contraceptive. Progestin-Plus is easy, dependable *and* reversible . . .'

'Is *that* you,' I go, 'rollerblading?'

Sahara's like, 'No, wait.'

'Progestin-Plus guarantees maximum safety *and* more bearable periods, offering *you* greater peace of mind . . .'

'That's not you bungee-jumping, is it?'

'No. *Ssshhh!*'

'So why not talk to your physician or healthcare provider about Progestin-Plus . . .'

'And that's obviously not you talking,' I go.

Corey goes, 'Ross, that's a man's voice.'

'That's why I said it obviously *wasn't* her?'

She's like, 'Oh my God, here it comes.'

We all automatically lean forward in our chairs.

A woman's voice – the fastest I've ever heard – goes, 'Must be fitted by a qualified medical practitioner. Candidates for Progestin-Plus are in a stable relationship and have no risk or history of ectopic pregnancy or pelvic inflammatory disease. Progestin-Plus does not protect against HIV or STDs. Ovarian cysts may occur and typically disappear. Complications may occur from placement. Accidental expulsion may result in loss of contraceptive cover. Missing periods or irregular bleeding is common in the first few months, followed by shorter, lighter periods.'

When it's finished, Nia and Corey give her, like, a round of applause. I *don't*, of course, because I'm seriously pissed off. I feel like I've been brought here under, I suppose you'd have to say, *false* pretences?

Corey's like, 'Oh my God, Sahara, this is only, like, the start for you?'

'Yeah, this time next year,' I go, 'it'll be rubber johnnies – you mork my words.'

But it's like they can't even hear me.

Nia's suddenly all Tyra Banks, clicking her fingers and flicking her head, going, 'You nailed it, Girlfriend!'

Then Sahara's old pair ring to congratulate her and Sahara tells them she thought about how she was going to do it for, like, *such* a long time and in the end decided to do it in exactly the same way as she did the disclaimer for Bank of America.

'If it ain't broke . . .' Nia goes.

This continues, it has to be said, for most of the next hour, until Corey eventually stands up and announces that she has, like, bikram yoga in the morning. Nia leaves as well, presumably not wanting to be a Klingon. On her way out the door, she tells me she hopes I'm proud of Sahara and I tell her of course I am – birds who can read fast don't come along every day.

I'm not a happy bunny, it has to be said, feeling like I've been taken for a mug here. But it's amazing how quick I am to let bygones be bygones when her friends are out the door and it's just me and her alone.

Not to put too fine a point on it, I'm all over her like I'm a diabetic and her tongue's sugar-coated.

She kicks off her flip-flops and drags me down onto the corpet. I yank up her structured Roland Mouret sheath – she told me what it was and how much it cost when she heard what she *thought* was a rip – then I'm suddenly showing her one or two tricks, which, judging from the oh-my-god tally, she definitely hasn't seen before.

Now this is going to sound weird, roysh, but despite all of this, I suppose you could call it, foreplay, it's pretty focking quiet south of El Paso. Which *never* happens to me. It might have been all the talk of pelvic inflammatory disease, not to mention stable relationships, but I'm suddenly limp as the proverbial bizkit.

Sahara *is* gagging for me so, all credit to her, she's pretty understanding in the circumstances. She suggests we take it through to the bedroom and just take our time. Which works a treat, as it happens. Five minutes of rolling around in the old Thomas Lees and she's suddenly taking the Lord's name again – this time at, like, the *top* of her voice?

At some point in the proceedings – I'd like to say halfway, but then I never make promises I can't keep – Sahara's face goes all serious and she's like, 'Fuck – what was that?'

I'm there, 'I didn't hear anything,' which I actually didn't?

But then, of course, I suddenly do. A man's voice going, 'I saw the TV! Congratulations!'

She says something then that always ends up nearly stopping my hort, no matter how many times I've heard it down through the years. 'Oh my God – it's my boyfriend.'

Of course, I'm out of that bed like the mattress is on fire and my orse is catching.

I'm going, 'Boyfriend? *Boyfriend?*'

She says he's supposed to be in Napa – as if that's *any* explanation.

'You never said you'd an actual boyfriend,' I go and she's there, 'Would it have mattered?' and I'm forced to admit – to myself obviously – that it never has in the past.

I'm telling you, if getting dressed running was an Olympic sport, Jockey Shorts would be banging the door down to sponsor me. I'm throwing on my clothes while she's rubbing her temples going, 'I need to think, I need to think, I need to think . . .'

However much time that's going to take, we actually don't have it? I jump into the old Dubes, then I reef open the window and look out. We're, like, two storeys up.

'I've got an idea,' she suddenly goes and, like a fool, I wait around to hear it.

'I'm really, really sorry,' she goes. 'You're, like, a great guy? But Trevion also happens to be my agent?'

I'm actually there thinking, Trevion? How random a name is that? when, all of a sudden, Sahara switches off the light on the nightstand, sending the room into total darkness, then storts screaming.

It all happens pretty quickly after that.

The next thing I hear is these big clumpy footsteps running across the landing, while at the top of her voice she storts going, 'Trevion! Trevion! I think there's someone in the room!'

The door flies open, the main light goes on and I'm

suddenly stood there staring at this enormous dude with biceps like focking basketballs. 'Who the fuck are you?' he goes, obviously surprised to see me.

I'm like, 'Okay, I kind of *know* how this looks?'

Sahara points at the open window. 'He must have climbed in,' she goes. 'Thank God you came home! I don't know *what* he was going to do to me.'

'Whoa, whoa, whoa,' I go, then I look at Trevion. 'I know it's no consolation to you, Dude, but this was an actual legitimate pull.'

Now I know fock-all about American sports, roysh, but I'd bet ten squids to your fifty that the thing that suddenly hit me across the side of the head and sent me falling against the wall was, like, a softball bat. My ears are suddenly ringing, but they're still working well enough to hear him tell Sahara to call the cops, which is when I realize that the time for, like, polite negotiation is over. The LA focking PD, I'm thinking, I've seen some of their work on YouTube.

I turn around and look at the drop to the ground. It's got to be, like, twenty feet, maybe more. But Trevion swings the bat at me again, this time missing my head, but taking, like, a huge chunk of plaster off the wall. I hop up onto the window-sill and, without even turning to Sahara to say goodbye, I jump two storeys to the street below.

2. On the shores of Lake Ewok

She's standing at the door of my hotel suite with a box of doughnuts and that smile that I never *could* resist? 'Peace offering!' she goes, waving them at me.

Of course, I'm not even that pissed off. But I'm still like, 'You were out of order – and we're talking bang.'

I let her in.

She goes, 'It's, like, oh my God, you have no idea how much of a shock that was to my system? But I totally over-reacted and I'm sorry.'

I tell her not to sweat it – it's LL Cool J.

'I've been trying to get her on her mobile,' she goes, as in Erika, 'but it's going straight to her voicemail.'

I'm there, 'I'd, er, leave her if I were you. I was talking to her – as in, yesterday? She said she doesn't want to talk to anyone. She mentioned needing space.'

'But she couldn't be including me in that. I'm, like, her Best Best Friend.'

'She said everyone.'

'But did she name me specifically?'

I just nod, which I suppose still counts as a lie. It's just I know that if the two of them get talking, *she'll* be on the next plane over and the next thing they'll be doing the whole sisters-in-law routine. I need time to get my head around this shit first.

I change the subject, tell her she looks well. She looks down and tells me it's a Brette Sandler sheer tunic and that *everyone's* going to be wearing them this year. And underneath she mentions that she's wearing an Ashley Paige bikini. I tell her I wouldn't mind checking it out, to see is it suitable for an establishment like this, and she laughs and tells me I'm *actually* dreaming.

'Anyway, get dressed,' she eventually goes, 'I'm taking you out for the day –*my* way of saying sorry.'

I grab a quick Jack Bauer, then we're suddenly on the freeway on the way to wherever it is we're going. We're in *his* old cor – the focking Prius – so I'm just sitting back, watching the sights. In the next lane, this – if I'm being honest – Alessandra Ambrosio lookalike in a Mercedes SLK Luxury Roadster gives me the serious once-over and from the look on her face, she's impressed.

'So,' Sorcha suddenly goes, possibly copping it, 'how was your date last night?' at the same time trying not to sound *too* interested.

I'm there, 'Not bad – I've *had* worse,' and she smiles and goes, 'Worse than a belt across the side of the head?'

She misses fock-all, in fairness to her. I touch my left temple. He could have killed me, the focking lunatic. She gives my hand a squeeze, to tell me she's only ripping the piss, and of course I end up *having* to laugh?

'So come on,' she goes then. 'Erika – tell me the story.'

I'm there, 'Not a huge amount to tell. Turns out my old man and her old dear were, like, childhood sweethorts . . .'

'Helen and Charles – oh my God, that's, like, *so* random.'

'Big-time. It's, like, who knows *what* the fock she saw in him.'

We end up stopped at lights. She goes, 'Your parents have had, like, *such* fascinating lives, haven't they?'

I'm there, 'Depends what you consider fascinating.'

'Like, I knew your mum was engaged before? Then that broke up and, well, she's told me loads about her Paris years. You know she had an affair with a bullfighter?'

thermogenesis, and the ones that contain *the* most pivotal thermogenic agents internationally studied.

Then I thought, what the fock, and for the last couple of days I've been taking all three. The upshot of that is that I smell like a dead mouse rotting behind a skirting board and as I'm standing here I'm having to clench every muscle in my lower body to keep my orse shut.

Moussaka probably wasn't the smortest idea in the world either.

The next thing, roysh, Ginnifer spots a friend of hers from reiki and it's weird because it's at that exact moment that I spot, of all people, Cillian, up at the bor. I'm there, 'I'll tell you what, you go talk to your friend,' giving her the guns, but without taking my eyes off him, 'and I'll come looking for you later.'

It turns out that Cillian's with Josh and Kyle. Josh is telling some bullshit story that involves the line, 'We're being *raped* on these derivatives,' and you can tell he loves saying the word.

Cillian doesn't even realize it, but he's, like, ten seconds away from being decked. I'm there, 'Who the fock are you telling Sorcha to get a court order?' but he actually shushes me, roysh, without saying even hello first, then tells Josh to continue, which of course he needs no invitation to do. 'I told him, "Hang tough, Dude!" Which he did.'

Cillian's there, 'And?'

He just smiles, then just goes, 'Fourteen *fucking* million,' and makes, like, a whooping sound. Then he turns around and bumps chests with Kyle, then with Cillian, then with a fourth dude who's there – a big fat focker with greased-back hair – who turns out to be Bob Soto, as in Cillian's boss at PwC.

I'm just, like, staring at Cillian. He's still got his swipe card from work attached to his belt loop. No one ever got laid wearing a swipe card – Rossism number two hundred and twelve.

I'm there, 'I asked you a focking question.'

'Wait a minute,' this Bob Soto dude goes, sticking a big sausage finger pretty much in my face. 'Who the fuck is *this* guy?'

What I *should* do is grab his focking finger and snap it back – but I don't. It's nice to be nice.

'It's Sorcha's ex,' Kyle goes and he's got, like, a little smile playing on his lips.

'This is him?' Bob Soto goes. 'This is *the guy*?'

I'm there, 'Yeah, what the fock is it to you?' and he sort of, like, pats me on the back and goes, 'Nothing. Really,' like there's shit he *could* say, but he's not going to?

I turn back to Cillian. 'Of course, you're loving it,' I go. 'The whole Starbucks thing. It's your chance to get me off the scene. Well, I can tell you this for a fact – it's not going to work. Honor's my daughter and nothing can change that fact.'

'You ever heliski?' Josh suddenly goes.

It totally throws me. I'm like, 'What?'

'We're going heliskiing next weekend,' he goes. 'Up to the Bugaboos,' and then he holds his hand up for Kyle to give him the least deserved high-five I've ever focking seen.

'Oh, *I* ski,' I go, 'don't you worry about that.'

Josh is like, 'I thought rugby was your thing,' and Bob Soto's immediately there, 'Rugby? Isn't that the game George Bush played in college?' and it's obvious what he's doing – he's trying to make out that I'm automatically a dipshit as well.

I just point at Cillian and tell him that if he thinks I'm going to let an actuary come between me and my daughter and, I suppose, my wife as well, he's got another thing coming.

Then I wander back to Ginnifer. She's still talking to her

friend, who it turns out is called Suzette and who seems cool enough, even if she's not the best looks-wise. When Suzette heads for the shitter I bring up the subject that's been hanging around the edge of the conversation all night. I tell Ginnifer I like her dress. She says it's a Kate and Kass halter. I tell her I'd love to see how it matched the corpet in my penthouse back at the Viceroy.

'Nice,' she goes, smiling, obviously appreciating a goy who knows how to talk the talk. 'Unfortunately, I've got to check on Picasso, my pygmy cat?'

'Oh,' I go, thinking it's an excuse.

She smiles. 'What I'm saying is, why don't *we* go to mine?'

I don't need to be asked twice. She doesn't even stick around to say goodbye to Suzette. Five minutes later, we're in an Andy McNab on the way to Whitley Heights.

Now, I've had my share of beautiful women over the years – and a lot of other people's share as well – but I have to tell you, I've never been so gagging for someone in my entire life. Even though all we're *actually* doing is holding hands, I've a nightstick on me that could put manners on a G7 protest.

I'm also clenching my orse cheeks like my life depends on it.

I suppose I should know how this evening's going to end when I hop out of the cor and pay the driver and get a sudden savage cramp in the old Malcolm.

There's one in the post – that's as sure as my eyes are focking watering here. I consider trying to maybe squeeze it out before we go inside, but Ginnifer's standing right next to me.

She puts the key in the door and shows me in. The gaff is actually a really nice little house – I remember what she said about being into, like, interior design? – and I realize it would be, like, the height of disrespect to open my lunch in here.

'Have you got, like, a jacks?' I go. 'In other words, bathroom?'

thinking I could drop it in there, then open the window and sort of, like, waft it out?

She's there, 'You'll have to use the upstairs one. I've just got through painting the one down here.'

She points up the stairs. 'It's the door immediately in front of you.'

The door immediately in front of me. I'm staring up at it. All I've got to do is get to the other side of that and I'm suddenly free from pain. I take the steps two at a time. But of course, in all the excitement, I let my orse muscles relax halfway up and without warning a fart nearly rips my orse in half.

There are no words you can say in that situation.

But there's also no way to describe to you the shock I get when I turn around to see Ginnifer lying in what would have to be described as a crumpled heap at the bottom of the stairs.

'No!' I end up shouting. It's all very *The Young and the Restless*. 'No!' and I leg it downstairs to check, I suppose, if she's still alive.

As luck would have it, she is – she's still breathing, even though she's out of the game. I whip open the front door and the cab driver is just turning the cor around. I call out to him and I tell him not to move. Ten seconds later, I come out of the house, carrying Ginnifer in, like, a fireman's lift. I lie her down on the back seat and I sit there cradling her head the whole way to the hospital, going, 'Hang in there, Baby! Don't you dare die on me!'

The driver asks me what happened and I tell him it's a long story.

'What's that smell?' he goes.

I'm there, 'Just put your focking foot down, will you?'

When we get to the hospital, there's nothing *but* questions.

They put Ginnifer onto, like, a trolley and as they're wheeling her along they're going to me, 'Did she take something? Drugs, maybe?'

I'm there, 'No.'

'Alcohol?'

'One or two cocktails. Three at the most.'

'Is she pregnant?'

'All I know is not by me?'

'Is she a diabetic? Is she allergic to anything? Penicillin?'

I stop walking with them and I'm suddenly like, 'Enough with the questions already! I *know* what happened. I . . . I farted and knocked her out.'

It's, like, the entire focking hospital goes quiet, then suddenly bursts out laughing. Everywhere, roysh, people are repeating what I said, then Ginnifer's taken through a set of double doors that I'm not allowed to pass through, but I'm told she's in, like, the best possible hands.

I wander over to the waiting area. I ring Trevion, but he doesn't answer. It *is* the middle of the night. I leave him a voicemail saying sorry I haven't been in touch. I'm in, like, the emergency room of the Cedars-Sinai. Ginnifer's been taken in, blahdy blahdy blah.

Then I get chatting to this really cool homeless dude with cirrhosis and I end up spilling my guts out to him, a total stranger. 'She played, like, a nurse in *House*,' I'm going. 'I'm not sure if that's actual irony, but it certainly feels like it should be. Jesus, she had, like, her whole life in front of her . . .'

After maybe twenty minutes, half an hour of this, Trevion comes bursting through the doors into the emergency room. He totally flips, which I knew he would. 'What happened?' he wants to know.

I shake my head. 'I knocked her out cold with one of my farts.'

'What?'

'Hard and all as that is to believe. I'm rancid at the moment.'

'She's out cold?'

'Yeah.'

He shakes his head. 'She's fucking narcoleptic, you idiot.'

I'm like, 'She's what?'

'It's a sleeping disorder. I told you before you took her out the last day.'

He did mention something, now that I think about it. 'Oh. I thought narcoleptics were the ones who can't stop stealing shit.'

He looks mad enough to put me through the focking wall. 'What are you two doing out anyway?' he goes.

'We went out on, like, a date?'

'A date? I told her to stay away from you.'

'Look, I'm sure she tried. But I rang her up and asked her out, just to say sorry for, like, ruining her career as well as my own. I actually really like her.'

'Oh, you do?' he goes, cracking on that he's actually happy for us. 'Aw, ain't that something.'

'Yeah,' I go. 'And I *very* seldom get serious about birds . . .'

His expression suddenly changes. He goes, 'Life's a fucking party for you, huh? Big focking jamboree . . .'

'No.'

'You eat tonight?'

'What?'

'You take her for a meal?'

'Yeah, as it happens. Le Petit Greek.'

'What you have?' he goes, looking at my, I suppose, midriff. 'Tell me it was stuffed grape leaves.'

'To stort I had, like, hummus, but then also Greek meat-balls because there wasn't a lot in it. If I'm being honest, I would have had some – probably most – of Ginnifer's feta salad as well,' and as I'm rhyming off all of this stuff, roysh, he's doing, like, calculations in his head, presumably working out the calories. 'For the main, I would have had moussaka, then one or two lamb kebabs, which I can never resist.'

Whatever bottom line he arrives at, he's not a happy camper. 'What are you, Elvis?' he goes.

I actually don't know what to say. I end up going, 'So who are the ones who can't stop stealing shit, then?'

'I don't *give* a fuck!' he goes, then marches over to the nurses' station. I hear him say Ginnifer's name, then the nurse mentions some shit about tests. 'She don't need no fucking tests,' he goes. 'She gets attacks of sleep. Mystery fucking over. Now go get her.'

He whips out his phone. He dials a number and the next thing he's going, 'Marty, it's Trev. Hey, I'm sorry for waking you. I got a story and it's all for fucking you, Bernstein . . . Yeah, that's it – you go *get* your fucking laptop . . .'

He puts his hand over the mouthpiece and tells me, totally out of the blue, that he doesn't *give* a shit about me anymore because today he signed a new star – a *real* star.

I'm there, 'Who?'

He just goes, 'Fyon Hoola O'Carroll-Kelly!'

Then he's back on the phone again. 'Yeah, Ginnifer Battles, you know her? *One Tree Hill. House.* You got it, Starsky! I'm here in the emergency room with her . . . Yeah, she nearly fucking died tonight. Choked on a Kalamata olive – can you believe that? Le Petit Greek . . . Larchmont, that's right . . . Hey, I'll find out . . .'

I'm beginning to think he was only ever using me to get to the old dear. It was probably him who told her to call me an idiot.

He turns to me. 'What was she wearing?'

I'm still in, like, shock, although I still manage to go, 'A red Kate and Kass halter dress.'

'You get that? Kate and Kass . . . Yeah, red . . .'

He turns to me again. 'Shoes?'

I shrug. 'It never came up.'

'Fornarina red heart peep-toe courts,' he goes, without skipping a beat. 'And the bag was a white Mulberry Alana . . . Friends said she's happy just to be alive – all that shit. Write it up . . .'

When he gets off the phone, I go, 'My old dear? How the fock did that come about?'

He's there, 'I picked up the phone. I said you got something, Kid, and I want to work with you.'

I'm there, 'So where does that leave me?'

He goes, 'All washed up, Starry Eyes. I couldn't even call you a has-been. You're a never-was.'

4. This is my comeback, girl

According to a poll on the internet, I'm the most hated man in America. Second in the world after Osama bin Laden and just ahead of Kim Jong-il, whose nuclear ambitions have apparently raised the spectre of annihilation for the planet. So I'm in the scratcher, roysh, shocked by this and, I'd have to say, even depressed.

I'm lying there also thinking, was that it? Was that really my moment of fame? I should have enjoyed it more, even for the seven days it lasted. I can suddenly understand why all these stars end up going focking bananas when no one's looking at them anymore.

I flick through the channels and find, like, an entertainment one, torturing myself I suppose. Because Amy Smart portied with fellow celebs Sandra Oh and Camilla Belle at the Foley + Carinna store opening in LA last night and even Sienna Miller was spotted enjoying herself in Foxtail looking fabulous in a Viktor & Rolf shirtdress with Sergio Rossi eel-skin pumps in blue.

I'm going, 'Enjoy it while it lasts, girls. Enjoy it while it lasts.'

Then, suddenly, up comes this photograph on Fox News that has my eyes out on actual stalks. It's a woman, roysh, totally naked, but painted from head to toe – including all of her various bits – in gold paint.

I'm actually lying there thinking it's one of the sexiest things I've ever seen when all of sudden I realize that it's *her* – as in the old dear? – and the old Malcolm does a quick lurch.

I have to turn up the sound.

'Now,' the newsreader dude goes, 'she's already the golden girl of women's fiction – now Fionnuala O'Carroll-Kelly is set to become the golden girl of marketing. The controversial writer – from *Ireland* – has been painted from head to toe in gold paint for a role in a commercial for Midas – a new brand of canned Prosecco. A warning to viewers that the following report contains *bodhrán* music . . .'

I don't focking believe it.

It comes on. It storts with, like, a picture of a leprechaun and – the dude's right – skiddly-eye music in the background. 'According to Irish mythology,' a bird's voice goes, 'the leprechaun is a type of male fairy who, many of the country's famously simple people will tell you, acts as a custodian for the pot of gold . . . contained at the end of *every* rainbow.

'Like the fabled creatures so beloved by Ireland's idiot people, Fionnuala O'Carroll-Kelly has shown that she, too, has the golden touch. *Karma Suits You – States of Ecstasy*, her steamy bodice-ripper about an Irish woman who experiences a sexual reawakening after coming to America, has topped the *New York Times* bestseller list for three weeks. And now Midas, a drinks company marketing a new brand of canned Prosecco, are banking on the fact that the stunningly attractive author . . . is worth her *weight* in gold.'

Then it switches to this dude with, like, a goatee? The caption says he's Richard Schor – Product, Promotion and Brand Executive, Midas. 'Fionnuala O'Carroll-Kelly is fresh, she's perky, she's effervescent,' he goes. 'But she also possesses a certain class and sophistication. The self-same qualities we associate with Midas Canned Prosecco. So in terms of matching a product *to* a star? This is what we would call a perfect strategic fit . . .'

'What he perhaps forgot to mention,' the report goes, 'is another quality they have in common – a great body . . .'

Whoosh. Up she comes on the screen, wearing half-nothing.

A focking bag of cement in a bikini. She's standing in what looks like an ort studio with all these, like, cameras and lights spread about the place and they're painting her – I shit you not – with, like, a paint gun?

'In the Irish language, Gay Lick, Fionnuala means, literally, white shoulders. Turning her into all-over gold was a job that took a total of six hours . . . *and* a lot of patience. First, they used a compressor gun loaded with liquid gold to give her body a first coat. A second and third were later added. Artists also used a special liquid gold leaf to colour her hair . . . while glitter varnish and eye shadow were painstakingly applied . . . to her nails and eyelids.

'Once the paint job was completed, Fionnuala had to remain deathly still – something that the highly driven author of three bestsellers back in her native Emerald Isle is unused to doing. And here – begorrah and be-to-hokey – are the results . . .'

They show her, like, fully painted, pulling various ridiculous poses in front of the camera.

'Fionnuala, who once posed naked for a Yummy Mummy calendar back in the Land of Saints and Scholars, was delighted with her new look, which is expected to adorn magazine spreads and billboards right across the country . . .'

They show her, like, afterwards – the focking whelk – with all the shit washed off her, going, 'Yes, it was wonderful fun. I've always said, *as* women, we should never be ashamed of our bodies – we *should* flaunt them more. Especially in later years. Like good Prosecco, they improve with age,' which was obviously totally rehearsed.

Then they show, like, one of the photographs of her in

all the muck again and the reporter goes, 'Midas will certainly be hoping that this Gay Lick Goddess helps them unlock the secret . . . *of* alchemy! Jess Cook, Fox News, *in* Santa Barbara.'

I straight away grab my phone. Trevion answers on, like, the third ring and I'm straight on the attack. 'I can't believe you let her do that. She's sick in the focking head. And *you're* taking advantage of that.'

'Hey,' he goes, 'quiet down, Tinkerbell – what do you want?'

'What do I want? What do you think? How would you like it if I painted *your* old dear and stuck her on TV?'

'She looked a million dollars up there.'

'She looked like she'd fallen off the top of a sumo wrestling trophy.'

'You know who I had on the phone today? Nous Model Management – mean anything to do you?'

I'm there, 'Not really.'

'Same crowd handles Paris fucking Hilton. Yeah, that's right, Smart Mouth. They're all over your mother. Offering her all kinds of work. I got Columbia on – can't wait to get her in the studio.'

'Studio?'

'They want her to make a record. Here in LA. Meanwhile, I can't move in my fucking office for all the shit that's getting sent to her. Shoes. Dresses. Bags. You like ladies' dresses?'

'No.'

'I think you do. I think they get you off.'

'They actually don't?'

'Yeah they do. My phone ain't stopped ringing. I got Marc Jacobs on one, Tony Burch on two, Zac Posen on three. They want to see her in their shit. I got a list of shows want her to cameo. *Ugly Betty. Desperate* fucking *Housewives*.

Everyone wants a piece of your mother and you want to know why?'

'Go on, enlighten me.'

'Cos *she* ain't you.'

'Exsqueeze me?'

'Hey, you heard it, Ladylove. She ain't you. She don't sit around getting fat and pissy. And remember this – she *done* something for *her* fame. Yours fell in your fucking lap and you still never knew which way was up.'

I'm there, 'Well, I would have thought in, like, a five-minute report there would have been *some* mention of the fact that her son happens to be Ross O'Carroll-Kelly.'

'Who?' he goes. 'Who's that? Never fucking heard of him. I got a newsflash for you, Friend – your mother's a star. You? You're nothing. You're last month's celebutard.'

You've no idea how actually hurtful that is to hear. 'Well,' I go, 'what if I told you I wanted to make, like, a comeback?'

He actually laughs.

I'm there, 'I'm serious. How do I get back up there again? I'm actually only realizing now how much I want all that shit – the clothes, the record deal, the whole blahdy blahdy blah.'

He tells me he's too busy with his real stars. I tell him I'll do anything he wants.

I've got, like, a roomful of people staring at me like I'm some kind of monster.

'You did *what*?'

And this from a dude called Snake, who's just admitted pimping out his wife for heroin.

'I gave my baby daughter a double espresso,' I go, shrugging my shoulders and trying to make it sound less of a big deal than it apparently is.

'You give me one good reason,' Bret, this sort of, like, trailer-trash dude, goes, 'why I shouldn't go over there and punch you into a twenty-year coma.'

Coke and gambling are Bret's bag. He sold his mother's gaff to pay off some bookie in Reno. She was still lying in her bed when they threw it out into the focking street.

'Bret,' Priscilla goes, 'one thing we don't dispense here is judgement – remember that?'

Bret takes a deep breath. 'It's just, you know, I got kids myself . . .'

Addiction Education was, like, Trevion's idea? He thought it might play well with the press, but I'll be lucky to get out of here with this pretty face intact.

This bird called Hazel (painkillers and surgery) says she recognizes my boat, then this Filipino bird called Dalisay (shoplifting and cybersex) says she saw me in a magazine. 'Giving that little girl coffee,' she goes. 'Laughing, real ugly,' and then all of a sudden Bret loses it again. 'You ever give my daughter anything,' he goes, jabbing his finger in my direction, 'be it a cappuccino, a macchiato, whatever – I will, *personally*, beat you unrecognizable with a fucking tyre iron. God fucking help me!'

'Let's control that anger,' Priscilla goes. 'Just visualize yourself back in that cell in Carson City and remember the breathing exercises we learned.'

Jesus Christ!

Priscilla turns to me then. 'Okay,' she goes, 'if we might take what I like to call a client-centred approach with you – what do you think was at the root of this behaviour?'

It's like being back in detention with the focking Jesuits – except there's no pulling the Senior Cup cord in here.

'Was it low self-esteem? Focal anxiety? Maybe simple insensitivity to the conventions of appropriate social behaviour?'

I'm there, 'I think it was simply the fact that she *wanted* coffee? If you knew her mother ... Even though, I've noticed, she's become more of a tea person since she came to the States.'

'Piece of shit,' Hazel goes – meaning me – and I look around, roysh, at the other faces and I realize that I've got to get out of here. To be honest, roysh, the only reason I even came was so the paparazzi could get a shot of me on the way out.

According to Trevion, people love a comeback story. But this crowd aren't loving *my* story and I'm sensing that my life is in serious danger here.

Priscilla wants more, though. 'Tell me,' she goes, 'about some of your close, interpersonal relationships?'

Shrinks, I know from personal experience, are like lions or tigers or any of that crew – throw them the odd bone and they'll generally leave *you* the fock alone.

'My home situation is pretty focked,' I go, then I notice Bret and one or two of the other men straighten up in their chairs. I wouldn't say they're on my side yet, but they're definitely prepared to hear me out.

I'm there, 'My old man, for instance. He's a dickhead and I won't give him the pleasure of even talking about him. Except to say that he had, like, a daughter – in other words, Erika – who he kept a secret for, like, twenty-and-whatever years . . .'

This bird Jennie (compulsive disorders and crystal meth) goes, 'Man, that is fucked up!' and suddenly I feel like I'm in an episode of *Maury*.

I'm there, 'I've been trying to tell people what a dick he is for years, but no one listened. So Erika gets wind of this – that *he's* her actual old man – and she ends up not even hating his guts. She's even calling him Dad . . .'

'That's not right,' Bret agrees.

139

I stare into the distance. 'The thing is, this bird Erika – *before* I knew she was my sister, I hasten to add? – I would have, you know, once or twice . . .'

'Ain't no shame in that,' Bret goes.

I suspect there probably isn't wherever he comes from. It's not the kind of thing I want bandied around the Merrion Inn, though.

'If I'm being honest,' I go, 'I'd say she's possibly the most attractive girl I've ever laid eyes on.'

Hazel goes, 'Don't you go blaming yourself. It's *his* fault – your father.'

I'm there, 'In many ways, I wish he was in this room to hear you say that.'

Hazel's there, 'No wonder you gave your baby coffee – you ain't in your right mind.'

I'm there, 'Exactly. I wish my ex-wife could see it like that. She's banging on about court orders and all sorts.'

Suddenly, everyone in the room wants to share.

'My ex-wife's a bitch,' Bret goes.

'Mine's a prostitute,' Snake goes, 'slash exotic dancer.'

By the end of the meeting, roysh, they're all on my side. Bret even apologizes for earlier – the tyre iron, blahdy blahdy blah. He says he's been pretty wound-up since the police seized his fighting dogs.

I'm thinking, I've always had, like, a way with people. 'Anyway,' I go, standing up, 'you've heard enough of my tales of woe . . .'

'Your agent's right,' Harvey goes. 'You *could* do with losing some weight.'

This is us in Newsroom on Robertson, finally getting that coffee, although what I'm actually drinking is one of these Taiwanese Milk Teas that he's been banging on about – I suppose just to show him that I *am* open-minded, even though I think he's accepted that nothing's going to happen between us.

'It's weird,' I go, rubbing my hands up and down my body, 'because in Ireland, this would be considered pretty much ripped.'

He pulls a face as if to say, sorry to disappoint you. 'You've got, like, a little cellulite,' he goes. 'Don't take offence – two or three weeks, we can work it off you.'

I'm flicking through his training journal and I can't believe the sessions he's putting in. 'I have to tell you,' I go, 'I was pretty proud of what I was bench-pressing until I read this.'

He tells me that I have to decide, from the outset, what my fitness goals are and I tell him I want abs like focking grill morks.

'Well then,' he goes, 'let's get to work,' and the next thing we're tipping across the road to the gym.

This is, like, step two of Trevion's plan to, what he calls, refloat my career.

I start off with, like, twenty minutes on the treadmill, then a few weights. 'It's always a good idea to rotate muscle groups as you work out,' Harvey goes. 'Or alternate, if you can, between cardio and lifting? It gives your muscles more time to rest. *And* it keeps your routine from getting monotonous.'

I tell him I wish I'd had him with me in Andorra. There were one or two guys on the team could have done with a good fitness coach.

He holds my two legs while I do, like, a hundred sit-ups. I ask him how his weekend went – because there *is* that whole getting-to-know-each-other vibe?

'Mike and I got in, like, a huge fight,' he goes.

I stop mid sit-up and I'm like, 'Who's this Mike?' but not

in, like, a jealous way. Again, I'm more making conversation than anything.

Mike turns out to be some dude who's been dicking him around for a couple of years. He's married, roysh, but he's been stringing Harvey along with the promise that he's going to one day leave his wife for him. Except if you ask me, he's obviously not. A player always recognizes a player.

'He was supposedly leaving her in April last year,' he goes. 'Then again in September. Then again last week. But when it comes to it, there's always something. "She's having a hard time at work." "Her sister's not well." "Let me just get through Christmas with her." And all this time I believed his bullshit. He's never going to leave her.'

I shake my head, do another ten sit-ups, then stop and go, 'Dude, do you mind if I say something to you? You let people treat you like that, they're never going to respect you. Take it from someone who's been dicking birds around his entire life.'

He rolls his eyes. 'Ross, this is nothing I haven't heard before.'

'Well, I'm just saying, I'd imagine you could do better. You know, you're actually a good-looking goy . . .'

Even that doesn't cheer him up.

'Do you mind me asking,' I go, 'how old are you?'

He's there, 'Twenty,' which actually surprises me, roysh, because I thought he was maybe twenty-four, twenty-five. I think I actually laugh. 'Twenty?' I go. 'Why do you want to be settled down at twenty? Especially with someone dragging *his* baggage – what, a marriage break-up? Harvey, you're just a kid – you should be out there breaking horts, loving it, loving it, loving it.'

He smiles, in fairness to him.

142

I'm like, 'Twenty? If you only knew the craic you're going to have in the years ahead.'

He shrugs. 'It's just that Mike was my first relationship,' he goes.

I'm there, 'A goy of your age shouldn't even know that word. Okay, when I break up with someone, especially someone I like – my wife is just one example – I always ask myself one question: was I happy the day before I met her? So, like, were you happy the day before you met this Mike dude?'

'I guess.'

I give him the guns. 'Then you can be happy again.'

He laughs, finally, and tells me I have a good perspective on things.

I do another fifty sit-ups straight and end up putting in, it has to be said, an unbelievable session – the kind I haven't done since I was at school. Practically every muscle in my body is hurting at the end, which is all good.

Even Harvey has to high-five me, as if to say, you worked today – respect.

We grab a quick Jack Bauer – yeah, together. That's how much it *doesn't* actually bother me? I even borrow some of his Ein Gedi Organic Dead Sea Mineral body scrub.

As I'm towelling off, I check my phone and notice that I've got, like, fourteen missed calls from Sorcha.

I'm there, 'Uh-oh.'

Harvey's like, 'What's wrong?'

'Sorcha,' I go. 'You remember her from the shop?'

He's like, 'Yeah, she's, like, *so* pretty.'

'Well, she's talking about getting some kind of court order out against me.'

'A court order?'

'Ah, it's not as big a deal as it sounds. It's possibly even for the best. It was all getting a bit weird anyway.'

He storts rubbing moisturizer into his body. 'How was it weird?'

'I suppose the big thing is that she doesn't seem to want me anymore,' I go, checking myself out in the long mirror. 'Not in *that* way.'

'Did you tell me she's with someone else now?'

'See, that wouldn't have stopped her in the past. There were, like, loads of times when she tried to move on, but I always managed to get back in there. The thing is, I think this time she really *does* see us as just good friends?'

'But that's good, right?'

I'm there, 'Is it?' stepping into my boxers. 'I mean, you've seen us together. All she wants to do is bring me shopping and talk to me about celebrities and fashion. I mean, don't get me wrong, I don't mind the odd time her asking me – just for the sake of argument – do these black Balenciaga trousers go with this Stella McCortney tailored blazer? Or even just, do these Kasil jeans suit me? You know, I've no problem saying, actually, yeah, the adjustable side buttons help prevent gaping at the back, thereby presenting a longer, leaner leg . . .'

Harvey cracks his hole laughing. 'Yeah, I would say you've spent *way* too much time shopping together,' he goes.

Of course, then I have to laugh as well.

He goes, 'So who does she usually shop with back home?' and I feel instantly guilty.

'Her best friend,' I go, 'as in her best *best* friend would have to be a bird called Erika. They've been bezzy mates since they were, like, thirteen.'

He's there, 'Maybe she's just confused. She's got this new guy, then you're suddenly back on the scene and she's still trying to work out how you fit into her life. So she's trying to turn you into a surrogate for her best friend.'

'No,' I go, 'she's trying to turn me into one of these metro-sexuals. No offence.'

He looks at me like he hasn't a bog what I'm talking about. 'Er, none taken,' he goes.

I'm there, 'See, my whole line on metrosexuals is they're basically men *as* women would have created them. As in, they're sensitive to women's feelings, carry bags, remember birthdays, never piss in the sink. It took women basically thousands of years to fashion this ideal man – then they discovered they didn't actually fancy him?'

Harvey breaks his orse laughing and I mean *really* breaks his orse. He tells me I'm the funniest person he's ever met, which is a huge compliment, it has to be said.

I finish getting dressed, then I tell him I better see what Sorcha wants. From the second she answers, I can hear the panic in her voice. I'm there, 'Sorcha, what's wrong?' but she can barely get the words out.

'I drove up to Tarzana to see that shop – the one that does Susana Monaco, Sass & Bide and Thread Social,' she goes. 'And *some* Elizabeth and James. The one that you were *supposed* to come to with me . . .'

I'm there, 'Well, I didn't think we were even talking, what with the thing about the coffee, the court order, blahdy blahdy blah . . .'

'I heard all this shouting and I looked across the road and these – bastards! – were surrounding this hairdresser's. They have her trapped in there, Ross . . .'

I'm there, 'Sorcha, who?'

She's like, 'Britney.'

I'm like, 'Britney?'

Harvey even mouths the word, 'Britney?' his face full of concern.

Sorcha's there, 'I'm standing looking at her through this

hairdresser's window . . . Ross, she's shaving all her hair off.'

I'm there, 'Shaving her hair off?'

Harvey puts his hand over his mouth.

I'm like, 'Are you sure it's her, Babes?'

'I think *I'd* know what Britney Spears looks like,' she pretty much roars at me.

'Sorry,' I go. You have to when they're like that.

She's there, 'It's the paparazzi – they've driven her to this,' and then I hear her going, 'Leave her alone, you vultures! That's all you are! Actual vultures!' and it's obvious that Britney's not the only one who's lost it.

There's suddenly silence on the end of the phone for ten, maybe fifteen seconds, then suddenly the kind of scream I haven't heard from her since Saoirse Bannon pipped her for the Mount Anville Student of the Year award thanks to the casting vote of Sister Aquinata.

'Oh my God,' Sorcha goes, 'she's, like, totally bald . . .'

'She's totally bald,' I tell Harvey. He puts his head in his hands. There's a focking pair of them in it.

The next thing, roysh, Sorcha must try to push her way past Britney's security – you've got to say that for the Mounties, they're focking defiant – because I hear her go, 'Don't touch me! Do *not* touch me!' and I immediately feel sorry for whoever the poor focker is. 'I've been worried about Britney since she tripped and almost dropped Sean Preston coming out of New York's Ritz Carlton,' she's telling them.

The next thing, roysh, I can hear this noise go up and my guess is that Britney's coming out of the place.

'Britney,' I hear Sorcha shout, 'we share the same birthday!' which is actually news to me, then a few seconds later, 'I just want you to know that I'm thinking about you and praying that you get well.'

When she eventually talks to me again, it's only to tell me that Britney didn't even look at her. She's bawling her eyes out, going, 'She didn't even look at me, Ross – not even once.'

'They're back together,' Erika goes and I end up nearly dropping the phone.

I'm there, 'Who?' except obviously I already *know?*

'Charles and my mum,' she goes. 'They've picked up where they left off.'

I'm there, 'Picked up where they left off? What, thirty years ago? That's focked up.'

'Ross,' she goes, 'that's my mother and father you're talking about.'

'Er, *yeah?* But that's, like, ancient history. Back to-focking-gether! What are they, sixteen? Can I just ask, have you actually seen this?'

'No. I don't want to see *her*. Dad told me . . .'

Again with the *Dad*.

'He came to the hotel today,' she goes.

'I take it you're still in the Merrion. I wouldn't focking blame you.'

'He says he loves her and she loves him. He says they never stopped loving each other.'

'Never stopped?' I go. 'Oh, the things I'm going to throw at that focker next time I talk to him. I'm actually going to sit up all night tonight making a list . . .'

'Ross,' she goes, 'do you think it'd be okay to ring Sorcha now?'

I'm there, 'No way. The, er, shit she was saying about you yesterday. I was like, "Whoa, that girl used to be your actual friend." I think it'd do more horm than actual good.'

'Oh,' she goes. She sounds pretty devastated, in fairness to her.

'And the next time you're talking to *him*,' I go, 'is there any chance you could remind him that he's still married to *my* old dear? Just in case it's slipped his mind.'

'Donald Faison loves this place,' Trevion goes. 'Jennifer Morrison, too. Jennifer's here *all* the fucking time . . .'

He's talking about Republic, this pretty rocking steakhouse in West Hollywood, where the nosebag's supposed to be incredible. Except I wouldn't know. I'm having a plate of focking hedge-clippings – though Trevion's pork three-ways with truffle fries and cheddar mac *does* smell incredible, in fairness to it.

'I'm going to have to take out earthquake insurance on you,' he goes – actually *happy* with me for once?

I'm there, 'Really?'

He's like, 'You better believe it. One or two people already calling you the next Coe Lynn Farrell – how do you like that?'

I have to be honest with him. 'Where I come from,' I go, 'he'd be considered a bit of a knacker?'

I'm chopping away through *my* plate like Indiana focking Jones. 'Let me tell you something,' he goes, waving a piece of pork at me on the end of his fork, 'there ain't nothing plays like contrition. Addiction counselling was a masterstroke. Martha Stewart's on the TV this morning – says we ought to show compassion and understanding . . .'

'Wait a minute,' I go, 'are you saying that the public love me again?'

He laughs. 'No,' he goes, 'I ain't saying they love you. I'm saying they fucking hate you a lot less than they did last week.'

'I suppose that's something.'

'That internet petition, calling on the Government to put you in Guantánamo . . .'

'Guantánamo? Isn't that for, like, I don't know, terrorists and that whole crowd?'

'That's right, Carlos. But only three hundred new signatures yesterday. That's down from *seventeen* hundred the day before. Just to give you a little perspective here.'

I nod, *trying* to see the bright side. 'It's hordly hero-worship, though, is it?'

'Hey,' he goes, 'you ever spend sixteen days in a trench up to your fucking neck in rainwater?'

I'm there, 'No,' even though he already *knows* the answer?

'See, that's why you never learned patience. But you will, Pilgrim. You will.'

I'm sitting there, staring at the big, scaly head on him, thinking, seventy-five! Maybe I should I stort listening to him more. The shit he must have seen in his lifetime. And I suppose he is entitled to be a bit grumpy, with a face like a focking baseball glove.

'Anyways,' he goes, 'I got you some movie work.'

My mouth just drops open. I'm there, 'Movie work? Are you serious?'

'Did you hear me laugh?'

'Er, no.'

'It's a kiddies' movie,' he goes. 'American football.'

I'm there, 'Whoa. So what am I – like, the coach? Because I can definitely bring something to that role.'

'Slow down, Sinatra. They're looking for a body double. No one's going to see your fucking face. Let me ask you something – you say you can kick a ball, right?'

I actually laugh. 'Er, you could say that.'

'Well,' he goes, 'that's all you *got* to do – they want to film your feet kicking the ball through the posts. The director's

Chubby Waghorne – a personal friend of mine. And speaking of chubby . . .'

He sort of, like, looks me up and down.

I'm there, 'What?' genuinely meaning it.

'What are we going to do about you?' he goes. 'You're getting fatter?'

I'm like, 'Fatter? Dude, I put in an unbelievable session in the gym yesterday. Look at me, I'm living on plants and focking shrubs here.'

He's there, 'I want to see you walking Zuma Beach, hand in hand with Katharine McPhee, Elisabeth Rohm, Demi Lovato. *Friends say she's never been happier. Thinks she's found the one . . .*'

'That's exactly what I want.'

'You take *that* body onto any beach on this coast, you take my word for it, Big Guy, Greenpeace are gonna drag you in the fucking ocean . . .'

'That's horsh.'

'It's true.'

'But there's not a lot more I can do . . .'

He stares at my body and, with a cheese knife in his hand, draws imaginary cut marks on my chest and stomach. I tell him no way. No *focking* way.

'Bit of lipo.'

'No.'

'Abdominal sculpt.'

'I said no.'

'Everyone out here gets work, Friend.'

'There must be another way. Harvey, an actual gay friend of mine, was telling me there's, like, firming gels?'

He shakes his head. 'Kid, forget about firming gels.'

'But they tighten up the blood vessels to give your muscles a more toned appearance . . .'

'Will you forget about firming gels already?'

He practically roars it at me. Everyone in the restaurant stops talking and stares in our direction.

'Forget! About! Fucking! Firming gels!' he goes again, through gritted teeth this time.

He looks away, roysh, like he's disappointed with me. Then, totally out of the blue, he goes, 'You know your mother was photographed in Susie Cakes this morning – yeah, with Marcia Cross.'

It's like, holy fock! I've a thing for Marcia Cross – a major thing.

He's there, 'That's right, Kermit. They're friends now . . .'

I know what he's doing. He's very subtly letting me know that he has influence in this town.

'Matter of fact,' he goes, 'she's coming to Fyon Hoola's reading tomorrow night.'

'Reading?'

'Yeah, she's reading in Book Soup. Famous place on Sunset. Everyone's going to be there. Not only Marcia. Kim Cattrall. Diane Kruger. Ziyi Zhang . . .'

I'm there, 'It sounds like things are really happening for her.'

'You bet they are. Because she's prepared to do whatever it takes. *She's* had work, you know.'

I laugh. 'I know that. She's had her face lifted that many times, she's practically wearing her orse as a hat.'

'That's why she's fast becoming one of the biggest names in showbusiness . . .' he goes.

There's no doubt, he knows what buttons to press.

'And you,' he goes, 'will always be just her son.'

'Okay,' I hear myself suddenly go. 'I'll do it. Whatever it takes.'

His face is even uglier when he smiles. 'We're going to get you a beautiful body,' he goes. 'I'm going to take you to San

Sancilio. He's from Ecuador. He's a personal friend of mine. He's not a butcher . . . He *was* a butcher, but he ain't a butcher now. No, now he does plastic – best in the fucking business.'

She smiles at me through the screen door. 'Oh my God,' she goes, 'I was just about to have my dinner.'

She's got one of those, like, Weight Watchers meals in her hand, which presumably is about to go into the microwave.

'Low in calories, high in misery,' I go, which is, like, an old joke of ours.

She laughs, then she throws her orms around me and says she's sorry about the whole Britney thing. I tell her it's cool. It must have been hord for her to watch – as, like, a fan? Hopefully she'll get the treatment she needs now that she's hit rock-bottom.

'Speaking of which . . .' she goes. And she smiles, you'd have to say warmly. 'I heard.'

She's obviously talking about me going to addiction therapy. I give her the line that Trevion fed me about having to face up to my actions.

She's there, 'That's, like, oh my God, Ross – I am *so* impressed.'

I'm thinking, after all the shit we've been through together, we're always going to be in each other's lives – even if it does have to be just friends.

She tells me to come in, then leads me through the huge hallway down to the kitchen. I can't help but check her out. She looks incredible in this black-and-white-striped tank top, which I'm pretty sure is the Daftbird one she mentioned Victoria Beckham was wearing the other day coming out of Shizue Boutique.

I say fock-all, though.

She puts her Storvation Chicken in the microwave and asks me what I've been up to. I tell her I spent the day hanging out with Harvey.

She laughs.

'Oh, the big bromance,' she goes. 'What, did you get, like, a manny-peddy?'

She *is* only joking, I should point out.

I tell her it was nothing as gay as that. We actually went rollerblading on Venice Beach. Harvey was teaching me.

She says she got a text alert this morning to say I spent the day yesterday playing tennis with Lo Bosworth at the Pacific Palisades Center. It said we were later spotted sipping bellinis in Shutters in Santa Monica, then dancing the night away in Opera on Schrader Boulevard.

I tell her it's total horseshit and I presume Trevion put it out there. 'I'm back in his good books,' I go. 'He's even got me, like, a minor movie role for tomorrow.'

She says she'd have been surprised if it *was* true because Lo and Lauren Conrad are, like, Best Friends Forever, maybe even Best *Best* Friends Forever.

I think she forgets that the Lauren Conrad story was horseshit in the first place.

Honor is sitting in her little play-pen, playing with a toy that's, like, fair trade, made from fully sustainable materials and completely and utterly boring. She drops it the second she sees me and storts stamping her feet up and down, her little face lit up like Tallaght on Christmas Eve.

I look at Sorcha, I suppose for permission, and she just nods and smiles, the whole coffee business totally forgotten, and I pick Honor out of her pen and carry her over to the island.

Honor's all excited, going, '*Eee, arr, san, ssuh . . .*'

I ask Sorcha what's that she's saying and Sorcha says she's counting in Mandarin. '*Hen hao*, Honor,' she tells her. '*Hen hao*,' then she checks her dinner to see if it's hot enough and goes, 'I'm not sure Lo Bosworth even *plays* tennis? She's certainly never mentioned it on the show. Although I heard she gets her highlights done in Juan Juan – the same place as me . . .'

I'm going, 'Honor, can you say, "Daddy"? "Daddy"?' determined that I'm going to hear her say something in English before her second focking birthday.

She reaches out her little hand and makes a grab for Sorcha's copy of *Karma Suits You – States of Ecstasy*.

'Oh no you don't,' I go. 'Coffee was one thing – porn is a complete other,' and, in fairness to her, Sorcha sees the funny side of it.

I tell her I can't believe she's reading this muck. She definitely shouldn't leave it lying around.

'Oh my God,' she goes, 'it's definitely her best yet. Your mum is *such* an inspiration, Ross – to all women. Emmy's only met her, like, once and she's already thinking of going back to UCLA to do gender studies.'

'Emmy?' I go. 'With the tennis orms?'

She's there, 'Yeah, she was asking all about you, by the way. I told you she had a thing for you.'

'But when did *she* meet my old dear?'

'Well, you know she's *in* LA now?'

'I heard. *I've* no focking interest in seeing her.'

Sorcha blows on a forkful of chicken. 'Well, we all went out for dinner – me, Emmy, Analyn, Elodine, your mum. They're all, like, huge fans, Ross.'

'You've got to be shitting me . . .'

She puts it in her mouth. 'We went to, like, Cut, this – oh my God – *amazing* steakhouse in the Beverly Wilshire, where Tom and Katie go *all* the time. Then we went to, like, Kress.

Oh my God, your mum was, like, bopping away with the best of them.'

'Spare me.'

'She was wearing this amazing Galliano babydoll dress. It was, like, lace? And, oh my God, she totally pulled it off . . .'

I shrug as if to say, I don't actually *give* a fock?

'She glitzed it up with, like, Lorraine Schwartz crystals . . .'

I stort playing the bumble-bee game with Honor, where you pretend that the tip of your finger is, like, a bee and you get it to, like, land on her nose. She actually loves it.

Sorcha's there, 'And she paid for, like, everything – which I was *so* mad at her for.'

'Ah, let her,' I go. 'She can do with all the friends she can get – even *if* she has to buy them . . .'

Sorcha finishes her dinner and pushes the little corton away.

I ask her, just randomly, how she'd feel about me getting together with Emmy, but she doesn't answer. It's like she hasn't heard me? I immediately cop that there's something on her mind. I know her almost *too* well?

'Go on,' I go. 'Spill it.'

She sort of, like, smiles – but not in a happy way. 'It's nothing,' she goes.

I'm there, 'Sorcha,' and I put my hand on top of hers, 'we've known each other a long, long time – and I'd like to think we're still friends . . .'

She takes, like, a deep breath, then goes, 'It's Cillian.'

'Cillian?' I go. I can feel my fists immediately tighten.

'No, it's nothing bad,' she goes. 'I'm just, I don't know, worried about him . . . Since he came back from heliskiing, he's been . . . different.'

'Different, as in?'

'Well, the night he came back, I was sitting down to watch *Nip/Tuck*. He walked in, muted the TV and said he was getting rid of the Lamborghini.'

I laugh. 'I wondered how long it would take,' I go. 'I knew it was too much cor for a goy like him.'

'Then he started talking about the subprime mortgage crisis . . .'

'Again? Can he not let it go?'

'That's what *I* said. But he's, like, totally changed his tune, Ross. He kept saying that the world economy was on the verge of collapse . . .'

Even I have to laugh at that.

'He said that the irresponsible lending practices of the banks, as well as the trading of risky debt obligations on the financial markets, meant that the entire world economy was built on sand.'

'So? What's that got to do with any of us?'

She's there, 'I don't know.' She looks like she's about to burst into tears. 'But then he started asking me how many credit cards I had and how much I owed on them.'

'Whoa – that's out of order.'

'He said we were all in the throes of a consumer binge that simply can't be sustained . . .'

'*Bang* out of order.'

'And he didn't mean just me, Ross – he meant, like, the whole world?'

'Did he snot himself while he was heliskiing or something?'

She nods. 'He had, like, a fall? Josh and Kyle said he had, like, a minor concussion? The doctor told him to just sleep it off. He got up the next morning and that's when it started. He's already cancelled our joint MasterCard.'

I have to bite my tongue to stop myself from saying I told

you so. This is what happens when you get mixed up with financial services heads.

'It'll probably pass,' I go.

She's there, 'I hope so. I mean, he walked into Bob Soto's office yesterday morning and said we were eighteen months away from a global financial crisis as grave as the Great Depression. Can you imagine, Ross – he said that to the head of International Risk Assessment in PwC!'

She's quiet for maybe thirty seconds. Then she goes, 'You don't think he could be right, do you?'

I shake my head. 'I'm going to be honest with you,' I go. 'I think Bob Soto's a dick . . .'

'Don't say that. He's been – oh my God – *so* understanding.'

'I think Josh and Kyle are dicks as well. But this I will say for them – they seem pretty confident of their shit.'

'That's what *I* thought.'

'Look,' I go, 'I'll tell you my whole, I don't know, psychology about the whole financial thing. I know fock-all about the economy and blahdy blahdy blah. But sometimes, if I'm flicking through the channels and I end up on the news and I see all those dudes on Wall Street, I just think, well, *they* obviously know what they're doing. That's something else I don't need to know anything about.'

She smiles at me. 'I love talking to you,' she goes. 'You make everything alright.'

Then she gives me an amazing – even if it is just a – peck on the cheek.

She stands up and puts her corton in the bin. She takes Honor out of my orms and says it's time a certain little girl was in bed. 'Say *buenas noches* to your father,' she goes. 'Can you say *buenas noches*?'

After a little bit of coaxing, she finally gets her to say the words.

'*Buenas noches*,' I go, although I'd much prefer to be saying goodnight.

As she turns to bring her upstairs, Sorcha mentions that she's thinking of hosting a fundraiser for the Jolie-Pitt Foundation, and I know immediately that it's the old dear's evil influence.

I'm having, like, a late brekky in the Viceroy when I decide to ring Christian. From the second he answers, he sounds pretty hassled. 'I take it she has you doing the middle-of-the-night feeds?' I go. 'You're focking worse to do it.'

Of course, it's only then that he tells me that I'm on speakerphone and that *she's* in the cor with him.

I'm there, 'Hey, Lauren, that was an actual joke,' except of course nothing comes back.

I carry on making the effort, in fairness to me.

'So how is he?' I go. 'They're focking great at that age, aren't they?'

Christian's like, 'He's, er, fine, Ross.'

I'm there, 'What are you even calling him?' half expecting him to say, I don't know, Jar Jar or probably Chief focking Chirpa.

'Either Edward Thomas,' he goes, 'or Thomas Edward. They're our grandfathers' names.'

Then I hear *her* go, 'Just hang up, Christian.'

Except it'll take a hell of a lot more than a bird to come between me and my best mate.

I'm quickly like, 'So where are you two off to?' recycling and going again. 'Dirty weekend somewhere?'

He's there, 'We're actually driving to Vegas. We're going to just live there on-site until the casino actually opens. There's so much work to do and, well, none of it's in California anymore.'

and utter contempt. 'Do you have *any* idea what it's like to lose your mind?' she goes.

I throw my eyes up to heaven. She's looking for sympathy now. It's no news to me that she's off her chops.

She's there, 'Have you thought about maybe showing some compassion?'

Her nose is running like a focking tap. I'm like, 'Compassion?'

'For the people involved.'

'Hand me my violin there, would you?'

'We're human, Ross – that's what you could never accept about your father and me. That's what you could never forgive.'

'Horseshit.'

'Yes. Imperfect people. And we made all the terrible, terrible mistakes that imperfect people make. But we tried to make the best of the mess we – all of us – created.'

'By letting Erika grow up thinking someone else was her old man? Yeah, *rul* nice of you. The thing is, I can't believe you actually stayed with him, even after you caught him dipping the wick . . .'

'Well, you're a fine one to talk about that,' she goes, staring at Sorcha's empty seat, *trying* to make a point? I decide to let her have her moment. But not for long.

'He's back with her,' I go. 'As in, Helen? I just thought I'd let you know that.'

But she already knows. I can't believe she already knows. Or that she doesn't seem to care. 'He loves her,' she goes. 'He's always loved her.'

'So why the fock did you stay together?'

'You don't know anything about the situation, Ross.'

'So explain it to me. Why don't you just . . . *explain* it to me?'

She doesn't say a word for ages. Eventually, roysh, she goes, 'I knew I got Charles on the rebound. We were *both* on the rebound. I'd been engaged myself . . .'

I'm there, 'Can I just say, I am actually stunned that there are that many desperate people in the world. But continue . . .'

'Your father and I met in Sandycove Tennis Club. It was the 1970s. And it was a terrible thing to be in your late twenties and on your own. For a woman anyway. We didn't love each other. But we liked each other and we had a lot in common. Tennis, for one thing. And maybe in our desperation we hoped that it was enough.'

'So, what, Helen came back from Canada, had a fling with *him*, got herself preggers . . .'

'It wasn't like that. I take my own share of the responsibility . . .' She dabs at her eyes. It's still her allergies. It's not tears, you can be sure of that.

I'm there, 'How?'

'I went through a couple of bad years. Almost lost my mind. My mother went loop the loop when she turned thirty and I was convinced I was going to go the same way. I drove him into Helen's arms . . .'

'You still haven't answered my question – why did he stay with you?'

'Because we had a six-month-old baby,' she goes, obviously trying to hang the whole thing on me. 'And we were married. And Helen was married, too. They were different times. Marriage was a life contract. It wasn't like switching phone networks.'

'So, what, it suited everyone to pretend it never happened?'

'I'm ashamed to say it, but yes. Your father and I decided to try to hold our marriage together. And I made his having no contact wth his daughter a precondition of taking him back. And I'm ashamed of that now. It was very, very wrong of me. But Helen had decided to go back to Canada. Tim said he'd raise Erika as his own. It suited everyone.'

'As long as no one ever found out the truth.'

'Yes.'

'It was the same with Ronan, wasn't it? Don't tell Ross he has a kid out there. Nah, just pay off his mother.'

'And that was wrong too . . .'

'Too focking right it was wrong.'

'You were *sixteen*. You were still a kid yourself. We did what we thought was right at the time.'

I sit up and take a good look at her. 'You sicken me,' I just go.

'I know,' she goes. 'But I'm hoping that one day you'll find it in your heart to forgive me. Just as you'll hope your children will forgive you for *your* awful, awful humanity . . .'

I'm thinking about Honor, whacked off her head on coffee, trying to horse that other kid's orm.

She goes, 'I'm hoping that one day you'll see that, on balance, given the problems we were presented with, we didn't do all that badly. I don't want us to go on hurting each other. I want us to be friends.'

Friends? She must have been at the vodka. 'You know, looking at you,' I go, 'I wouldn't blame the old man for going elsewhere for it.'

She smiles at me, roysh, but it's not a nice smile. It's, like, evil? 'And don't be jealous of my fame,' she goes. 'I *worked* for mine, remember?' which is about as low as you can possibly go.

'At least I didn't have to get half my orse fat injected into my lips,' is what I *should* say.

Except, like all the best lines, I didn't think of it until ages later.

*

183

So who, being honest, could put their hand on their hort and say they ever saw me in, like, a gay bor?

But I swear to God, roysh, there I am, sat with Harvey in Mother Lode in West Hollywood, the two of us drinking pink drinks with umbrellas and all sorts of accessories sticking out of them and playing a game that he calls P.S. Too? It basically involves watching men *and* women – because there *are* birds in there, don't you worry about that – and trying to decide who's had Plastic Surgery and who's, what Harvey calls, Factory.

So someone'll walk by, roysh, and I'll be there, 'Factory,' and he'll be like, 'You're kidding me, right? Those tits are, like, so P.S. Ross, they don't even match her arms!'

Then we end up getting busted. Some dude overhears us talking about him, walks over to us and goes, 'Wrong! I've had my ears done and a tattoo removed,' and he storts laughing, then we stort laughing and I can honestly say, roysh, it's the best craic I've had since I came to the States, and that includes all the birds I've scored.

'Hey, speaking of plastic surgery,' I end up going, 'I've decided *not* to go ahead with the whole body resculpt thing?'

He's there, 'Oh my God, why?'

They're all very dramatic, aren't they?

I'm there, 'Bottled it, in fairness. Went for the assessment and the dude storted drawing all over me, telling me all the shit he was going to do – rip this, peel that, chop the other. I ended up sort of, like, fainting?'

The dude just explodes – it's like it's the funniest thing he's ever heard? He's there, 'You fainted?'

Of course, I end up having to laugh as well.

'Yeah, I was out for, like, five or six hours. But I woke up and told Trevion, fock it, I'm going to keep doing the work in the gym – after that, the public are just going to have to take me as they find me.'

I ask the borman for two more pomegranate daiquiris.

Harvey goes, 'Good for you.'

I look around the bor. It has to be said, roysh, that if you walked in here off the street, you'd never know there was anything funny about it.

'This place is nothing at all like I expected,' I go.

Harvey rolls his eyes, which is another thing a lot of them do. 'Let me guess, you thought it would be, like, men in denim shorts, leather jackets and handlebar moustaches?'

I'm there, 'No,' even though that's exactly what I expected.

'I can bring you to one of those bars if you like,' he goes and I'm quickly there, 'No!' which he thinks is hilarious.

A dude walks by, bursting out of his shirt. 'Pectoral implants,' Harvey goes out of the side of his mouth, hordly even *needing* to look at him.

I'm there, 'Do you mind me asking you something? Like, when did you first know that you were . . . you know?'

'Do you mean *gay*, Ross?'

'Your word, but yeah.'

He takes, like, a sip of his drink. 'Thirteen?' he goes. 'Fourteen?'

I'm there, 'Wow,' really meaning it. 'See, the thing I'm always wondering is, how do you *actually* know?'

He's there, 'Well, with me, it was when I first started listening to my mother's Diana Ross CDs.'

'Really?'

'Ross, I'm joking?'

'Oh, sorry.'

'I don't know when or how I knew. I think I always just knew.'

I nod.

'Are you actually from, whatever, LA?'

'No,' he goes, 'but I'm from California? A town called

Barstow? It's in the Mojave desert, halfway between here and Vegas.'

'Sorry to, like, bombord you with questions,' I go, 'but I suppose I'm just curious. Like, did you *have* to come to LA, if you know what I mean?'

'Do you mean was I run out of town for being a homosexual?'

'Er, yeah.'

He laughs. I think he finds me one of the genuinely funniest people he's ever met.

'No,' he goes, 'I came to LA because Barstow didn't have much of a gay scene, that's all.'

I'm there, 'So what did your old pair say when you told them you were – exactly – gay?'

He doesn't answer, roysh, just stares at his drink. I'm thinking they must have taken it really badly and now I'm suddenly regretting bringing it up.

So I go, 'Do you mind me saying something to you, Harve?'

'No, what?'

'I really admire you. And that's not me being funny or anything? I've never met someone so, I don't know, comfortable in their own skin.'

He smiles at me and says thank you because, like, he *knows* I mean it?

It's at that exact point, roysh, that my phone rings. It's, like, a three-five-three number, so I answer it and it turns out to be Fionn, ringing from school. I don't know if I mentioned, but he's back working as, like, a teacher again?

'Ross,' he goes, 'I'm sorry to ring you so late at night.'

I'm there, 'Don't sweat it, Dude. At this precise moment in time, I'm sitting in – of all things – a *gay* bor, if that's okay to say. Would you believe me if I told you I've got – and you'll appreciate this more than anyone – a *gay* friend . . .'

I put my hand over the phone and go, 'Fionn's not *actually* gay? It's just a thing I've always slagged him about.'

Then I go back on the phone. I'm there, 'That's genuine, by the way – I have my first ever gay mate. And I'm completely cool with it, aren't I, Harve?'

'Except you keep mentioning it,' Harvey goes, 'like, every five minutes.'

'He's not one of the scary ones,' I go to Fionn. 'The ones where you'd always be thinking, if I was hammered, could I trust him?'

'Or trust yourself,' Harvey goes.

I'm there, 'Hear that Fionn? We're like Will and Jack here when we get going.'

Fionn's straight down to business. 'Is it true,' he goes, 'about Erika?'

I'm there, 'Depends – what have you heard?'

He's like, 'Ross, don't give me that. I met her in Dunne & Crescenzi tonight, eating on her own.'

I'm there, 'What was she wearing?'

He's like, 'What?'

I'm there, 'I mean, did she look well? Or healthy – did she look healthy?'

'Ross,' he goes, 'she looked like a broken woman.'

I'm there, 'Well, she's certainly playing the sympathy cord with you lot. And before you say it, I haven't turned my back on her. To be honest, it's, er, Sorcha – she's having serious trouble getting her head around the fact that Erika's suddenly my sister. As I said to Oisinn, give her time – she'll come around.'

'Have you told Ronan?' he goes.

The simple answer, of course, is no, but I end up getting in a bit of a strop with him? 'Sorry, how is this any of your beeswax?'

He's there, 'Well, I could say I'm asking you as Ronan's year head. I have an interest in his welfare. Or I could say that I'm asking you as a friend who actually cares about you.'

That hits me full in the chest. See, I never give the four-eyed focker the credit he deserves.

I'm there, 'Sorry, Dude – it's just been, you know, a bit mental even trying to get my own head around it.'

'Look,' Fionn goes, 'the story's already all over town. JP saw your old man and Erika's old dear coming out of the Bedroom Studio in Dalkey the other day.'

'That's *actually* revolting.'

'Whether it is or not, Ross, you should tell Ronan before someone else tells him.'

The dress code, she said in a text last night, was gorden party casual. I just threw on the usual chinos and Ralph, but when she cops me on the other side of the pool, horsing into a plate of zucchini custards with balsamic vinegar reduction, she checks me out, we're talking up and down, then mouths the words thank you.

Which is always nice to hear.

She doesn't look nervous, even though it's some turnout. There must be, like, two hundred people here, a load of them seriously rolling in it by the looks of them.

Of course, this is her in her element. I think she was born with a microphone in her hand.

'Hello and welcome,' she goes. 'And thank you for coming to what I hope will be the first annual Designer Clothes Auction (Including Vintage) in Aid of the Jolie-Pitt Foundation, which is one of the world's most – oh my God – amazing charities. Let me say at the beginning that fifty per cent of all monies raised today will go to the Maddox Jolie-Pitt organization, which is dedicated to eradicating extreme rural poverty, protecting natural resources and conserving wildlife by promoting sustainable rural economies that directly contribute to the health and vitality of communities, wildlife and forests . . .'

That gets an immediate round of applause. Did I mention that she looks amazing?

'The remainder will go towards helping children affected in various ways by the war in Iraq. Half will go to help military children through the Armed Services YMCA Operation Hero programme and half will go towards programmes that help Iraqi children sadly orphaned by the fighting.

'Obviously, Brad and Angelina can't be here today, but, as Angelina said herself in a recent interview with *O – The Oprah Magazine*, educational support programmes for the children of conflict are the best way to help communities heal . . .'

Everyone claps again.

'You know, she's even more beautiful than I remembered,' Harvey goes. 'She looks like Jennie Garth.'

I'm there, 'That's exactly what *I* used to think.'

I tell him that the nuns from that school of hers would be proud of her today. Public speaking was always one of her things.

The models stort coming out, except they're not so much models as all Sorcha's mates.

'Now, Barneys on Wilshire,' she's going, 'have donated this black, one-shoulder dress with bow detail by the fabulous Marc Jacobs. I think you'll all agree that Elodine totally pulls it off with this Touch Luxe silver scales jacket, Louboutin heels and – can we see the pin, Elodine? – a Lucite flower pin by Alexis Bittar, as seen in *Sex and the City*. And we're going to start the bidding for the entire ensemble at five thousand dollars . . .'

'And where's *he*?' Harvey goes.

I point over to the little group of them standing over by the actual buffet. Josh is throwing a bread roll like it's an American football and Kyle is running to catch it. I just shake my head. Aport from the fact that Sorcha paid good money to get this event catered, his throwing action is actually shit.

'Which one?' Harvey goes. 'Deion Sanders or Joe Montana?'

I'm there, 'Neither. The one sitting down. The pale, white, weedy-looking focker with the imitation Ray-Bans.'

He turns to me in, like, total shock. 'You lost *that* girl . . . to *him*?'

I'm there, 'I didn't lose her *to* him? Even though *he'd* like to think that. No, I was cheating on her left, right and centre. The nanny was the one I eventually swung for. Then he came in and hoovered up the pieces.'

'Now,' Sorcha goes, 'Kitson, one of my all-time favourite shops, on Robertson, have donated this ruffled Mulberry dress, which is stunning, I'm sure you'll all agree . . .'

I tell Harvey thanks, on Sorcha's behalf, and he just lifts his hand as if to say it's not a thing. 'Analyn is wearing it with these fabulous Alaïa pumps – lace-effect is going to be in this year – and an Orka Mesica friendship bracelet, as worn by Nicky Hilton, though in my opinion it would go equally well with simple flats, either Pierre Hardy or Rene Caovilla, and statement tights.'

Harvey gets up off his lounger.

'Where are you off to?' I go, but not in, like, a clingy way?

He's there, 'Are you kidding me? I've just mentioned the names of two sports people. I've clearly been spending too much time around you,' although, I should add, he *is* joking. Then he's like, 'It's a fashion show. Where do you think I'm going? To find cute gay guys.'

I laugh.

I'm just there, 'Good luck, Harve,' thinking how cool it

would be if he finally found someone nice – man *or* woman.

As he's walking away, roysh, I notice Cillian's crew staring over at me. Josh has his T-shirt rolled up, roysh, showing off his – I suppose – midriff and he's sort of, like, prancing around in, like, a gay way, basically ripping the piss out of Harvey. I actually feel like going over there and decking him. Kyle is laughing and sort of, like, slapping Cillian on the back, although he seems to be just sitting there, staring into space.

'The next lot,' Sorcha goes, 'is a soft grey, scallop-tiered dress by my favourite designer in the actual world – and that designer is none other than Stella McCortney . . .'

The model, in this case, is Emmy, as in Sorcha's friend? The one who, even Sorcha admitted, has a major thing for me. The opening bid is, like, two thousand doughnuts and my hand is, like, straight in the air, because, I have to admit, she looks amazing in it.

I've only got, like, one rival bidding against me and it's Bob Soto, as in Cillian's boss, the fat fock. He's over there with Josh and Kyle, then three or four dudes that Cillian obviously works with, because looking at them, I've seen more craic at an autopsy.

Bob goes to two and a half and I immediately say three and, of course, Emmy's little face lights up the second I up the ante. He puts his big fat sausage finger in the air to say three and a half. I give Emmy a sly smile, then I go to four.

I notice Josh and Kyle egging him on, telling him to blow me out of the water. He goes to four and a half, but I can tell from his whole body language that he knows – being in the business he's in – that the dress is worth nothing like that. And of course I'm like Harvey focking Norman here – I won't be beaten on price.

So the upshot is that he eventually drops out and I end up agreeing to pay basically six grandingtons for the dress, although that's *with* a pair of suede Manolos in electric-blue and a HK for Mouawad bracelet thrown in. Then I just lie back on my lounger, soak up the rays and wait for my prize.

A voice above me suddenly goes, 'Spending your money?'

I have to, like, shield my eyes from the sun. It's Trevion.

I forgot to mention, Disney still paid me for that movie.

I'm there, 'Actually, *yeah*, as it happens? What are you doing here?'

'I'm here with Fyon Hoola,' he goes. 'She's modelling.'

I'm there, 'Modelling? Modelling what?'

Sorcha's suddenly there, 'Kushcush have very kindly donated this stunning metallic silver monokini and it's being modelled by someone with whom I'm sure you're all very familiar – an amazing, amazing writer who I'm, oh my God, *so* fortunate to be able to call a friend, and no stranger to charity work herself, Fionnuala O'Carroll-Kelly!'

Out she focking struts, her big fat body bet into the focking thing. There's not only cheers, roysh, there's actual roars? It's, like, does anyone in this country have any taste?

Of course, I can't help myself. 'Someone stick an apple in its mouth and put it on the barbecue!' I shout.

Trevion doesn't even blink. He's just, like, staring at her. The poor focker's smitten.

'I should add that those amazing Jee Vice sunglasses are Fionnuala's own,' Sorcha goes, 'and not part of the bid.'

The old dear says something then – she *has* to be the centre of attention – Sorcha goes, 'Oh my God, thank you *so* much! Ladies and gentlemen, Fionnuala has very, very kindly agreed to throw in the glasses – and I think I'm right in saying that they're the same ones that Katherine Heigl was pictured wearing recently leaving the Christian Audigier Warehouse . . .'

I suddenly spot Emmy over at the ice-cream buffet. I get up, tell Trevion he's selling himself short – we're talking *way* short – then I tip over to her, giving her a big enthusiastic kiss on either cheek.

Of course, Bob Soto's taking all this in, totally bulling. If you can't hang with the big dogs, stay your puppy ass on the porch.

'Oh my God,' Emmy goes, 'I can't believe you paid all that money. And look, I'm eating sorbet in it! I should go and change.'

I'm there, 'Wait a minute – are you telling me *you* don't come with the dress?' which *sounds* corny but it's actually not, the way I say it. 'Dying kids or no dying kids, I'm afraid I'm going to have to ask for my money back.'

She's big into me and she's making it obvious, roysh, with the whole eye contact thing and then laughing at pretty much every line I throw at her. For instance, roysh, I tell her that tennis obviously suits her, judging from her body, then she asks me if I play and I tell her no, I'm not interested in games in which love means nothing. It's an old line, roysh, and one I've only ever known to work on Loreto Foxrock girls. But this is America – a whole new morket to crack. 'Oh my God,' she goes, her mouth wide open, 'that is *so* clever!' and what can I do, roysh, except shrug.

It's like, hey, I've got seven or eight lines just like that one.

Of course, you know the script. Twenty minutes later, we're in – funnily enough – the pumping house and we're up to our tonsils in each other. Emmy unbuttons my shirt, then we're suddenly rolling around on the filthy floor. She's keen, it has to be said – going at me like a dog with a focking chew-toy. We're pulling and ripping out of each other, neither of us giving a shit about the dress. If anything, roysh, knowing how much it cost actually adds an edge to proceedings?

Fifteen minutes later – or whatever – I finish up. We eventually get our breath back, then get to our feet and stort fixing ourselves, tucking ourselves in and whatever else. It's only then that Emmy mentions the dress. 'Oh my God!' she goes. 'Look at the state of me!'

I'm there, 'Who *gives* a fock?' feeling a bit Jay Z, if I'm being honest about it.

I'm looking down at the Manolos. The suede is, like, scuffed to bits and one of the heels has even broken off.

As for the dress, you wouldn't wash your focking car with it now. It's, like, shredded to pieces, especially around the orse, and covered in, like, dirt and oil and of course my mucky handprints. 'We shouldn't have done that,' she goes.

I'm there, 'Fock it, I'm, like, a celebrity now. Rock and roll! Blahdy blah!'

'It's not that,' she goes, 'It's just, Sorcha thinks you bought the dress for *her*.'

I could be wrong, roysh, but as she turns to leave, basically holding her various bits together, I think I notice the slightest trace of a smile on her face.

Much as I love women, I'll never fully understand them.

I make it back to the pool, roysh, in time to see Honor come out modelling a striped dress by Splendid Littles with Ryan Flex sandals by Pediped. It's the final lot of the day. Everyone's cheering, roysh, and she's loving being the centre of attention, going, '*Hola! Hola! Hola!*' and I'm thinking that I'm glad I didn't miss it – they're, like, the precious moments you can *never* get back?

My clothes are, like, filthy, so I end up hiding behind the hand-carved marble gazebo, trying to clean myself up, using a bottle of Club Soda and a piece of soft grey material that, in the throes of passion, I must have ripped from the dress.

That's where Sorcha eventually finds me.

The first thing she says is that she's been looking all over and I hide the piece of material in what would have to be described as a blizzard of movement. She doesn't even comment on the state of me and I immediately realize that she's upset. She throws her orms around me and, like, bursts into tears. I still suspect that this has something to do with Emmy and experience tells me to put one hand over my balls.

She eventually pulls away and goes, 'Steve and Elodine have gone home,' and I'm storting to relax, realizing that this might not be something *I've* actually done.

I'm there, 'What happened?'

She looks away. She says there was, like, a major fight. Everything was going *so* well until Cillian brought up the whole economy thing.

I shake my head. 'It's actually getting boring at this stage.'

'He said that the granting of mortgages to people who can't afford to pay them is going to set in chain a series of events that will drive the world economy to the point of collapse . . .'

I've just made shit of a six-grand dress. I don't want to be listening to this.

'He said the crash would be every bit as bad as 1929. Ross, what happened in 1929?'

I shake my head. 'Don't ask me. But I presume the rest of them weren't just standing there agreeing with him?'

'No,' she goes. 'Josh said that bad debts aren't necessarily a bad thing. He said it still makes sense to sign up riskier borrowers because, even with the increased rate of default, the ones who do pay will still generate greater profits for the banks and financial institutions than if the capital was lying there, like, unused?'

I'm there, 'See? That's that, then.'

'But Cillian said that assumed that the level of default can be predicted and managed. He said the good times would only last as long as the housing and employment markets

195

remain buoyant and people with steady wages are able to service mortgages on properties that are steadily increasing in value. He said that a contracting economy, combined with a fall in house prices and the resetting of mortgage interest rates from the original teaser rates offered, would result in an increase in foreclosures that – because of the greed of people like Josh and Kyle – would set the whole edifice of Western capitalism crumbling.'

'Look, I'm not a fan of those two,' I go, 'but it sounds to me like Cillian was bang out of order there.'

'Well, can you *imagine* how Steve and Elodine felt? They gave Josh and Kyle money to invest, Ross. What if they lose their ethnic restaurant before it even opens?'

'That's not going to happen,' I go, liking the way my voice sounds.

'I've had their taster menu,' she goes, tears streaming from her eyes. 'Their pigori are amazing. What if . . .'

'I said, that is *not* going to happen.'

'But how can you be so sure? Cillian told them that those CDOs they invested in were essentially IOUs that one day someone was going to have to pay. Or *not.*'

'How can I be so sure?' I go. 'I'll tell you how. Because when it comes to shit like this – world affairs, blah blah blah – I always go with whoever makes the least sense to me. And when I hear Josh and Kyle banging on about the economy, I genuinely don't understand a word of it. I rest my case.'

That seems to put her mind at ease.

Unfortunately, it doesn't last long. All of a suddden, roysh, a voice storts coming over the, I supposed you'd call it, a PA?

'We were sold a dream of prosperity,' it's going, 'but it was all based on chronic indebtedness . . .'

Sorcha's hands go up to her face. 'That's Cillian!' she goes, then she immediately turns and runs in the direction of the gaff, with me haring along after her.

He's nowhere to be seen. People are standing around with their glasses of Pims and their canapés and totally bemused looks on their faces, while his voice continues to boom out. 'The simple fact is we have been living way beyond our means,' he's going.

People are turning to Sorcha, going, 'This is *not* what we came to hear,' and Sorcha, of course, is apologizing to everyone.

'Cillian!' she's shouting, looking around her. 'Cillian, where are you?'

'Yes, despite all the warnings signs, we continue to run up unsustainable levels of debt to feed the media-driven consumption frenzy and acquire the things we've been led to believe constitute success . . .'

People are storting to drift away now. One woman turns around to Sorcha and goes, 'I pay six thousand dollars for an Oscar de la Renta original with Le Silla Swarovski sandals, then I get a lecture?' and she walks off, not a happy bunny rabbit.

'Once, the US economy was the envy of the world,' he keeps going. 'It was based on the principles of enterprise, ingenuity and hard work. America built things – things it could be proud of, things that withstood the rigours of time. But not anymore. Now it builds nothing. Instead, it glorifies people who simply move money around the place and do so with increasing recklessness . . .'

Josh and Kyle come pegging it over, out of breath. They say he's somewhere inside the gaff, although with the size of the place, it could take, like, an hour to find him.

'When the crash comes – and come it will – we will remember these as the years when our insatiable appetite for consumer debt met the stop-at-nothing practices of our banks and financial institutions. We will be picking through the debris for generations to come. When I close my eyes, I see redundancies, insolvencies, bankruptcies and home repossessions . . .'

Sorcha has, like, tears running down her face. 'Please,' she's going, 'everyone stay.'

Even the old dear, who's holding Honor, is going, 'Everybody – it's just someone who's had too much to drink.'

Honor's going, '*Buenas noches*,' and at the same time clapping her hands. '*Buenas noches*.'

Nobody's thought about doing the obvious. But it's one of those moments – cometh the hour, blahdy blahdy blah. I go over to the PA system and just, like, rip the plug out of the wall. There's suddenly silence, roysh, but at that stage pretty much everyone has gone.

Harvey, who's standing talking to this blond dude in a yellow Hollister T-shirt, says well done to me, which *is* nice to hear.

Then Sorcha pretty much collapses on my shoulder, so upset she can barely get the words out to tell me that people have left without their seed packet favours. I stare at the gaff, with that lunatic somewhere inside, and I think seed packet favours are the least of her worries.

'Hey, Ronan, where are you?'

There's, like, shouting in the background. Someone's calling someone a fock-ass motherfocker and then that someone says, basically, fock you, you focking fock.

It sounds like he's in Dr Quirkey's.

But of course Ro has a Good Time Emporium of his own these days. 'We're watching *Casino*,' he goes. 'Here, Buckets – hit pause on that thing, will you?' and the shouting suddenly stops.

I'm like, '*Casino*? You're already getting in the mood for Vegas, then.'

He goes, 'I'm after watching it eight times, amn't I, Buckets?'

'Eight times?' I go.

He's there, 'You wouldn't exist out here if it wasn't for me. Without me, personally, every motherfucker would have a piece of your Jew ass.'

'Maybe you should make this the *last* time you watch it?' I go, suddenly sounding like what I actually am, which is his father. 'Ro, I've got something I want to talk to you about. Don't worry, it's not bad. It's more . . . focked up. The thing is, you know Erika?'

He's there, 'Er, yeah.'

'Of course you do – you really like her, don't you?'

He's there, 'I love Erika,' and there's me forgetting how well they hit it off.

'Actually, that's probably going to make this a lot easier,' I go. 'The thing is, it turns out she's kind of your auntie?'

'Me auntie?'

'And it's *his* fault, in case you're trying to work it out – your focking hero.'

'Me grandda?'

'Exactly. He had a fling with her mother in the – whatever – old days. So the way it's set up now, she's, like, my sister?'

His reaction, I have to say, takes me by total surprise. 'That's great,' he goes, genuinely delighted.

I'm there, 'I mean, I know it's embarrassing – we're *some* family, aren't we?'

'It's great,' he goes. 'Here, get off the line, Rosser – I want to ring her.'

Talk about a conversation stopper. 'You ever read any Philip Roth?'

199

It's, like, where the fock does Trevion dig up these birds for me?

'*American Pastoral*?' she goes. '*Zuckerman Unbound*? Any of those?'

'No,' I go, not having a bog what she's talking about, but at the same time trying to *look* intelligent? Talking to birds is a bit like doing the oral Irish.

She's there, 'So who *have* you read?' actually wanting me to name books.

What I should say is, 'None – I'm still sexually active,' but I don't. Instead, I end up subtly changing the subject. 'Aisha,' I go, taking a whack of my appletini. 'That's a nice name – I presume it's after, like, the country?'

Birds named after countries *always* have chips on their shoulders. Birds named after months of the year have huge bazambas. Birds named after colours never wax their bikini lines.

'Country?' she goes. 'No, it's, like, the Stevie Wonder song? "Isn't She Lovely"?'

I shrug. In fairness, she *is* lovely, despite the attitude she's giving me. She actually looks a bit like Abbie Cornish.

We're in, like, Lola's in West Hollywood, this bor where they do, like, a hundred different martinis. Mine are all going straight to my head and I know deep down that I shouldn't be drinking them so fast.

Hindsight, blahdy blahdy blah.

Aisha asks me if I'll mind her bag – which is something I hate, by the way – because she's just spotted Maniche, who's *supposed* to be her sister's sobriety coach. Off she focks and, whatever, the two of them end up having what would have to be described as a heated exchange up at the bar which lasts, like, an hour?

Of course, bored off my tits – and this is going to *sound* bad? – I end up having a root through her Bottega Veneta knot clutch, looking for johnnies, if I'm being honest, because she's already mentioned that she has a kid and I don't want to end up paying vagimoney to a third bird for the rest of my actual life.

There's the usual shit in there – lotions, potions and mixed emotions. Then a picture of a little baby – presumably Coco, as in the daughter she's been banging on about? She looks about Honor's age. I wonder has *she* got any English yet?

But there's no zepps, roysh, although I do manage to find a packet of what are called Milktests. If you've never heard of them before, roysh, they're basically little breathalysers to tell birds who've had a few Bartons when it's safe to, like, breastfeed again?

I whip one out, open the little plastic package that it comes in, then give it a blow. The little strip changes colour and I check it against the code that comes with the instructions. It looks like Cardamom Yellow to me, which means I shouldn't breastfeed for, like, eight hours.

So what happens next is there's a crew at the next table, three or four dudes – jocks, roysh, but still sound – and they're all giving it, 'Hey, what's that thing you've got there?'

So I end up telling them and immediately, roysh, it's like I'm a God to these goys, in other words the biggest legend who ever lived? They ask me to come and join them, which I do, and of course then it's like, game on.

I throw the box of Milktests in the middle of the table and we order, like, a round of shots. They're all drinking Sambuca, so of course I end up going with that.

We knock our drinks back, as in skull them, then one of the dudes – he's a ringer for Zac Efron but it's *not* him? – blows a Tangerine, which is seriously impressive, in anyone's money. Don't feed for twelve hours! I'm second with a Pale Orange and the other three are all on Brilliant Saffron.

Of course, I love a focking challenge. I'm the guy who did the entire Alexander College Debs Committee – going through the cord, as we used to call it.

I order a tequila sunrise and also a baby Guinness, which gets a round of applause from the table. Even Zac Efron's giving me big-time respect. Straight down the Jeff Beck. Blow. Roars from, like, everyone. Cherry. Don't feed for sixteen hours!

The rest of them drop out. It's obvious this is, like, a two-horse race.

Zac Efron ups the ante. A gin rickey, then an Alabama slammer, which is, like, rocket fuel. I shake my head. No way. He knocks them back, one after the other, pulls a face like he might vom, but holds them down. Blows a Brilliant Vermilion. Do not feed for twenty-four hours!

I *have* to high-five him. No focking debates. Then I'm thinking that even though I'm in, like, another country, this is just like being back in Special Ks with the guys.

'I'll see you your gin rickey and your Alabama slammer,' I go, 'and I'll raise you . . . a zombie.'

There's suddenly what would have to be described as a collective intake of breath.

'You'll die!' Zac Efron goes. And he might be right. If I was a bird, my breast milk would already be, like, eighty-five per cent proof. The drinks arrive. My back teeth are focking floating. I grab the gin rickey – throw it down. I grab the Alabama slammer – throw it in on top of it. Then the zombie – get it into you, Cynthia.

Quick blow. Black! One of the goys is just, like, staring at the instructions. 'Oh my God!' he goes. 'Please consult your physician!'

Everyone just, like, cheers. Even Zac Efron makes, like, a sign with his hands as if to say, I'm out, dude, and the rest of them are going, 'Legend! Legend! Legend!'

I literally haven't experienced hero-worship like it since that day two months ago in Andorra.

All of a sudden, I happen to look up and who's standing over the table only Aisha, with a face on her like squashed cantaloupe. She snatches her bag, gathers up what's left of the Milktests and storms off.

The goys are all going, 'Man! You're in trouble,' and in normal circumstances I'd be like, 'Fock her – plenty more, blahdy blahdy blah,' but I actually fancy a shot at the title tonight.

See, birds with 'tudes have *always* done it for me?

So I say goodbye to the goys, then I chase after her. She's outside, trying to hail a Jo. 'One thing I'll never get tired of hearing,' I go, flicking my thumb in the direction of the bor, 'the applause of the crowd.'

She's *not* a happy plant-eating, burrowing mammal. 'There I am,' she goes, 'trying to talk sense into Maniche about her drinking, then I come back to find my date . . .'

She can't even finish her sentence. But she obviously wants me, roysh, because when a Jo finally pulls up, she gets in and leaves the door open for me.

It's only when I get in the back beside her that I realize how absolutely stupid drunk I am. And I say that just to let you know that anything that happened after that wasn't *my* basic fault?

We go to her gaff. Don't know where. Remember very little about it.

I do remember her yabbering away to the childminder in the kitchen, mostly about shite, while I was in the living room, like a good groundsman, testing the firmness of the sofa, the likely burn-factor of the corpet and – being a details man – the tensile strength of the coffee table.

It might have been all the waiting around, but I had a bat

in my chinos that could make Barry Bonds look like a Little Leaguer.

In she eventually comes, after letting out the childminder. Kicks off her Cesare Paciotti's and flicks off the light.

Of course, I'm straight out of my seat and all over her like an oil spill. She tastes of apple and boysenberry.

I'm actually unbuttoning my fly when she's suddenly there, 'Stop it! Wait!' and pushes me back onto the sofa.

'Let's take our time,' she goes. From somewhere she produces a box of matches and she walks around the room, lighting all these candles, which she has every-focking-where. 'Let's get the mood right,' she goes.

I crack on that I'm cool with it. She's obviously one of these I Have Needs Too freaks.

There must be, like, thirty or forty candles in the room and it takes a good ten minutes for her to light them all. But she does it without once taking her eyes off me and I have to say, roysh, it's seriously, I don't know, erotic looking at her boat race in the flickering light.

She crawls over to me on her hands and knees, a dirty big smile on her face. Then she hits me with it from out of nowhere.

'Do you like Satan?' she goes.

I'm like, 'Er . . . I'm pretty sure I misheard that. Lot of drink on board . . .'

'What do you think of Satan?' she goes again.

The last time I was asked a question like that was at Honor's christening, but that was cool because it was in, like, a church? But here I'm suddenly shitting myself and I can tell you, I'm sobering up fast.

'I'm not really sure I believe in messing around with that shit,' I end up going.

She's there, 'You'll give it a try, though – right?'

I'm there, 'Errr,' trying to think.

'Come on,' she goes. 'You'll love it. I promise.'

I'm there, 'But your daughter's in the next room.'

'She loves Satan.'

I try not to look too shocked, roysh, because inside my mind I'm suddenly planning my escape. 'Em, okay,' I go, playing it LL. 'I'll give it an old lash, then.'

Her eyes light up. 'Really?'

'As I always say, don't knock it until you've tried it.'

'Great,' she goes. Then she gets to her feet. 'I'll, em, go and get things started,' and she turns and heads for, like, the kitchen, presumably to get, I don't know, a crucifix or some shit?

The second she turns around, roysh, I'm up off the sofa like I don't know what and I pretty much launch myself at her. Now I've tackled some of the toughest in the business. Even Jerry Flannery will tell you that he's got, like, a permanent click in his hip from the time I held him up five metres from the line in a friendly years ago. But Aisha is surprisingly strong. I mean, yeah, she goes to ground pretty easily, as you'd expect, but she fights me back and manages to kick me full in the stomach, winding me for a few seconds.

She gets up, roysh, and tries to run, but I quickly ankle-tap her – the wily old pro – and she hits the deck again. Then it takes every bit of strength I have to drag her, biting and gouging, to this little cupboard beneath the stairs. I literally throw her in there and turn the key in the door.

She's going ballistic – and that's *not* an exaggeration? – calling me all sorts of names, some of which even *I've* never been called before.

'Well, what are *you*, then?' I'm going. 'You're a freak is what you are!'

'Let me out of here!' she's going, banging on the inside of the door.

I get out of there as fast as my legs can carry me. And it's maybe an hour later, when I'm back in the hotel, fixing myself a nightcap from the minibor, that I think about Coco, that poor little baby left alone in that actual house.

Because that's me. I'm an actual softie. I think about going back. Deep down, though, I know it's too dangerous. How long is that door going to hold her anyway? I decide that there's nothing else for it. When in doubt . . .

Trevion answers, sounding majorly cranky. It *is* four o'clock in the morning.

I'm there, 'Where the fock are you pulling these birds from?'

He's like, 'What?' obviously still only waking up.

I'm there, 'As in Aisha. I don't care who you owe favours to – I'm not dating any more lunatics.'

He's there, 'What are you talking about?'

'That bird – she's into, like, devil worship.'

He's there, 'Hey, slow down, Elmo. What are you talking about?'

I'm like, 'She kept banging on about Satan.'

'Satan?' he goes.

I'm there, 'Satan! She kept saying how she loved Satan.'

'Satan?' he goes. 'Are you sure she didn't mean seitan?'

I'm like, 'Satan – exactly.'

'No,' he goes, 'I mean *seitan*. With an ei.'

I'm there, 'Dude, Satan is Satan – no matter how you spin it.'

'*Seitan*,' he goes, 'is a kind of food.'

I suddenly feel my entire body freeze. It's one of those moments when you *know* you've focked up? You're just waiting to find out how.

I'm there, 'A food? What kind of food exactly?'

'Jesus, it's wheat gluten. Cooked. What the fuck does it

matter? Vegetarians eat it. Full of protein. Your wife had it at her party . . .'

I'm thinking . . . Actually, I don't know what I'm thinking. Oh fock definitely figures in the shuffle. 'No, no, no,' I go, 'she said she worshipped Satan.'

'Lot of girls do,' he goes. 'Especially if they want to keep the weight off.'

'She said she'd introduced all of her friends to it.'

'So?'

'She said it'd be Satan for breakfast, lunch and dinner if she had her way.'

'Are you done already?'

I'm there, 'Er, yeah,' at the same time thinking, Oh, fock!

'By the way, I need to talk to you,' he goes. 'You and Fyon Hoola.'

'Look, I don't want to be in the same room as that woman. What's it about anyway?'

'It's about fucking MTV, that's what. They want to meet you both. Tomorrow night. Chateau Marmont. Eight o'clock. You fucking be there, you hear me?'

I'm there, 'Er, okay.'

'Now let me get some sleep here.'

I'm like, 'Er, just before you go, Trevion. Back to the whole Aisha thing. Satan, blah blah blah. To cut a long story short, I locked her in a focking cupboard.'

He's there, 'You *what*?'

He does laugh, in fairness to him. Eventually.

'Which probably *is* out of order, looking back now. Is there any chance *you'd* swing by and let her out?'

I've honestly never heard her so down in the actual dumps. She says she's okay, but I've known her long enough to know when she's putting on, like, a brave face, even when it's over the phone.

'And how's *he*?' I go – not that I *give* a fock? Except that he *is* sharing a house with my wife and daughter.

She's there, 'Quiet. He hasn't got dressed for, like, three days.'

I'm like, 'Are you saying he hasn't even been to work?'

'Bob told him to take a couple of weeks off. He needs rest, Ross, but he's spending the entire time just reading. Constantly.'

I tell her that doesn't sound good, though she doesn't need me to point that out. 'Why don't you come and stay in my suite?' I go. 'And that's not me trying to get in there. It'd be separate beds.'

The thing is, roysh, I actually mean it?

'I really, really appreciate that,' she goes. 'But I can't just walk out on him, Ross. I think he's really unwell.'

'I'm just saying, the offer's there.'

She tells me that I'm – oh my God – *so* an amazing person and I'm actually feeling pretty good about myself until she mentions Erika.

'Ross,' she goes, 'can I say something to you? And please don't take this the wrong way because it has been, like, *so* great having you here? But . . . I really miss my best friend.'

I'm there, 'Give her time. I'm sure she'll ring you when she gets her shit together.'

'You know, I almost rang her today?' she goes. 'As in, I actually called up her number and hit dial? But then I changed my mind before she could answer.'

'I, er, wouldn't advise you make a habit of that. Like I said, she's pretty pissed off with you, for whatever reason.'

She sounds like she's out and about, by the way. I ask her where she is and she says she's in the cor, on the way to Emmy's.

I'm there, 'Emmy?'

'Yeah,' she goes. 'Oh my God, she's being *so* weird at the moment?'

I'm like, 'Weird, as in?'

She's there, 'Weird, as in she still hasn't given me my dress. She's not even returning my calls.'

I'm like, 'I, er, better go – I'm meeting Harvey for lunch.'

She goes, 'Oh my God, is it true that you and your mum are meeting some guy from, like, MTV tonight?'

I'm there, 'Er, yeah. I'm not exactly sure what it's about.'

'Oh my God, whatever it is, I would *so* love to be in it, Ross.'

I tell her I'll give her a shout later and tell her what it's about.

Harvey's sitting outside Café Midi with a couple of Tapioca Pearl milk teas. 'You certainly enjoyed yourself at the fund-raiser,' I go. 'What was his name?'

He laughs. He's got that look about him. 'Hugo,' he goes, except he can't say it without smiling.

We've all been there.

'He's a good-looking goy,' I go, which is an amazing thing for me to admit. 'He better not come between our friendship.'

He laughs and says he won't. 'You look like you've something on your mind,' he goes.

I shake my head. 'Do you ever get the feeling,' I go, 'that there's a whole heap of trouble heading your way?'

They're already stuck into the Châteauneuf de Plonk, the two of them. She's rubbing her hand up and down her leg, like she does when she's mullered and making a disgrace of herself.

'Look at the focking state of you,' I go. 'If a fisherman pulled you out of the sea, he'd throw you back.'

She doesn't say anything. And neither does *he* – except, 'Sit down, Gracie. And keep your mouth shut. It's listening time.'

I was actually about to sit down anyway.

He's like, 'How would you like to star in your own reality TV show?'

I'm a bit taken aback. I'm there, 'Whoa! Are we talking like *The Hills*?'

He shakes his head. 'We're talking like *The Osbournes*,' he goes. 'Like I told you, I been talking to MTV. One or two executives. Personal friends of mine. Obviously, they know all about your mother . . .'

They automatically smile at each other. I think he's actually in love with her, the poor focker.

'They was there that night in Book Soup,' he goes. 'They wanted to know was you for real . . .'

I'm like, 'Was *I* for real?'

He's there, 'Shut up. Are you kidding me? I said. The way this kid speaks about his mother! The way his mother speaks about him!'

I turn to her, a bit hurt to be honest. 'What bad shit could you possibly say about me?' She just blanks me.

'So I starts telling this guy your whole situation. Your boyfriend . . .'

'He's not my boyfriend.'

'Your wife and kid. That crazy fuck they're living with. And just generally how stupid you are – giving coffee to the baby, taking that girl to the emergency room because you blew gas in her face, yada, yada, yada. Let me tell you, the guy nearly pops his hernia this morning laughing at the sei- tan story . . .'

I'm there, 'I'm glad to hear I amuse someone.'

He's like, 'Yes, you do, Chico. Yes, you do. Let me tell you, this guy says to me, we got to get this family on camera. This is *Newlyweds* meets *The Hills* meets *Hogan Knows Best* . . .'

From the general vibe of the conversation, I know that I'm basically Jessica Simpson.

'They want to give us Johnny Sarno,' he goes. 'One of the best directors in the business. Twenty-five years old. He's on his way here right now. And let me tell you, he's pumped about meeting the two of you.'

I look at the old dear, then back at him. 'Have shekels been mentioned? I presume they have.'

'They want to pay you guys – fourteen half-hour episodes – Two! Million! Big ones!'

'Two million?' I go. I've suddenly got my business hat on. 'Wait a minute, are we talking dollars?'

'No, we're talking Twinkies,' he goes. 'What do *you* think?'

'Okay, I just thought I'd check. They always say, don't they, that you *shouldn't* just rush in and accept the first offer? But, having thought about it, the answer is yes, I accept.'

'You *accept*? Well, hoo-fucking-ray for Jay Gatsby.'

The old dear laughs, loving seeing me under pressure.

The next thing I see, roysh, is this Chinesey-looking dude – and, again, that's not racist – walking towards us with his hand outstretched and his mouth open wide in a look of what would have to be called awe. Trevion wasn't bullshitting – he obviously *is* excited about meeting me?

I stand up, shake his hand and tell him that if MTV wants to follow me around while I do my shit – scoring birds, drinking for Ireland and roaring general abuse at that dog over there – then I've no problems taking their focking money.

I turn to the old dear. 'Are *you* up for it?'

You'd want to hear her. 'Television is one medium I've always been desperate to get into.'

'Yeah?' I go. 'That and medium dress.'

Johnny turns to Trevion with a big delighted smile on his boat – what I'm beginning to realize is his normal look.

'Isn't it great?' Trevion goes. 'That's how they talk to each other, all the time.'

Trevion calls over the waiter and asks for another bottle of wine.

'Couple of questions,' Johnny goes. He talks with, like, a normal American accent? Presumably he was born here? 'First, what are you going to do with this thing?' and I swear to God, roysh, he actually points at my nose.

'What's wrong with my nose?' I go, naturally enough.

Trevion gets in on the act then. He's there, 'It's huge is what's wrong with it.'

The old dear has the actual balls to laugh.

I'm there, 'I'm not going back to that San whatever-he's-called,' and then I turn to Johnny. 'Did *he* put you up to this?' meaning Trevion.

'No,' he goes, suddenly staring at the middle of my face, taking it in from, like, various different angles. 'I think it would be distracting, that's all – draw attention away from the action.'

I turn to the old dear. 'Are you not even going to stick up for your son?'

She just shrugs and turns her head away. 'You got your father's nose,' is all she goes.

Trevion's there, 'I'll ring San. We'll get you booked in for a new one tomorrow.'

'No.'

'It's just your nose.'

'I told you, I'm not letting that lunatic near me.'

Johnny goes, 'No nose, no deal,' leaving me with no choice.

Trevion laughs. 'Hey, cheer up,' he goes. 'When you're

really in the big time, you think anyone's going to take out their coke with that fucking thing in the room?'

'I don't do coke.'

'Well, you ain't gonna be offered any either. You're like an anteater there. So the nose goes – no vote. I'll ring San. He's done rhino a whole heap of times. He could do it in the morning.'

'This is going to be on, like, TV. So the whole world is going to know I had, like, a nose job?'

'We'll tell them it was medical. You broke it playing . . . what's that shit?'

'Rugby.'

'Yeah, whatever. An old injury – never healed properly.'

'We could film the operation for the show,' Johnny goes, looking delighted. 'Also,' he goes, 'we want to get you all living under one roof.'

Trevion's there, 'I was telling him, your wife's got that big house, right?'

I'm like, 'Yeah, but I'm not sure I could handle living with that focking Cillian.'

'Well, that's the deal,' Trevion goes. 'Take it or don't. *Ross, His Mother, His Wife and Her Lover* . . .'

I look at Johnny. 'Yeah, that's what we want to call it,' he goes.

Trevion's like, 'And that's what they want – the whole dysfunctional lot of you, under one roof.'

He gives the old dear a smile of apology.

I'm there, 'Well, I'll have to ask Sorcha first,' and the old dear's suddenly looking over my shoulder, going, 'No time like the present.'

I don't even get a chance to look around. Sorcha's suddenly stood in front of me, with a face like a dick in a bucket of Deep Heat. It's obvious that I'm in serious shit.

213

Without saying a word, she throws a glass of wine over me – *my* glass?

'That,' she goes, 'is for having sex with my friend at my party . . .'

Trevion turns to Johnny. He's there, 'See what I mean?' and Johnny's just, like, nodding his head, again looking like the cat that got the focking cream.

Sorcha picks up the old dear's glass. That goes over me as well. '*That* is for doing it in a dress that cost six thousand dollars . . .'

Then she makes a grab for Trevion's and I'm thinking, shit, what else *is* there?

'And that,' she goes, throwing it straight in my face, 'is for lying about Erika not wanting to talk to me.'

Like I've said time and time again about the Mounties, they're dogged.

Then she just bursts into tears.

The old dear stands up, puts her orm around her and gets her to sit down with us. 'Can we get some water over here?' she shouts to no one in particular.

Sorcha's like, 'Red tea, if they have it.'

'Red tea,' the old dear goes. 'And another bottle of wine,' then she sort of, like, strokes her hair and tells her that everything's going to be okay – which she's never done for me, can I just say?

Sorcha rears up at me again then. It's like the end of a focking horror movie – you never know when they're really done, do you?

'You *know* how I feel about Stella McCortney,' she goes.

She turns to the old dear for support. 'Anytime I have, like, a really difficult decision to make, I'm always there, WWSD? As in, What Would Stella Do?'

'Are you sure it's Stella?' I make the mistake of going. 'As in, are you sure it's not me being with someone else that's upset you?'

It's definitely *not* the wisest thing in the world to say?

She looks at me in, like, a suddenly nasty way and goes, 'I just thought you might like to know, Ross, that she's coming over.'

I'm there, 'Who?' presuming we're still talking about Stella.

She's there, 'Erika.'

My entire body just goes cold.

'I booked her a ticket,' she goes. 'She'll be here tomorrow.'

Johnny, of course, is totally confused. 'Who's Erika?' he goes, looking from me to Sorcha to Trevion.

It's the old dear who goes, 'Erika is Sorcha's best friend. Ross just found out that she's also his half-sister.'

Trevion smiles so wide you could fit that wine bottle in his mouth sideways. 'What'd I tell you?' he goes. 'They make the Manson family look like the fucking *Brady Bunch*.'

6. A brand new face for the boys on MTV

Pumped and all as Sorcha is about being on reality TV, I think that, on balance, I probably owe her an apology, which is why I call out to the gaff the following morning with a tub of Edy's Slow Churned Rich and Creamy Cheesecake Diva ice cream as, like, a peace offering – the small one, I *should* add, because she's already banging on about how the camera adds eight pounds.

It turns out I've just missed her. Cillian says she just left for the airport, which means that Erika's going to be here in a couple of hours. 'I wonder how she'll look,' I hear myself go. 'Not great hopefully – long flight, lot on her plate, blahdy blahdy blah . . .'

He looks like shit, I should mention. He's still in his pyjamas – *pyjamas*, by the way – with four or five days of beard growth and a hum coming off him that tells me he hasn't showered in that time either.

He doesn't even ask me in. He tries to talk to me at the door and I have to, like, push past him with my bags and remind him that I actually live here now?

Then I ask him, nice to be nice, if he's looking forward to being on TV and he laughs – again, *if* it was a word – dismissively. 'I've no intention of involving myself in that frivolous rubbish,' he goes. 'Obviously, I can't stop Sorcha . . .'

'No, you can't,' I go, checking out his weedy little auditor body and making sure he *sees* me checking it out as well.

'But I've told her my feelings, that our obsession with surface details – like clothes and superficial celebrity – is going to make it harder for us all to come down. Now is the time to start appreciating the things that *are* important.'

'Deodorant obviously isn't one in your book,' I go – and even *I* have to admit that it's one of my best ever lines. Then I'm bulling, of course, that the cameras weren't here to, like, witness it?

He shakes his head. 'You really have no idea of the storm that's coming, do you?'

I'm there, 'All I know is, I don't think those mates of yours would have been out of order decking you at the Maddox Jolie-Pitt fashion fundraiser.'

'Josh and Kyle?' he goes, then he laughs. He's there, 'The wizards of high finance!' Except you can tell he doesn't, like, mean it? 'The financial sector – people like those two – they used to be the servants of the economy and we let them become its master. But who's been looking after the interests of society?'

I hope he's not waiting for an answer from me.

'Our political leaders,' he goes, 'here, back home – have you ever noticed the way they behave around men with money? Like silly girls. They're so besotted, they forget whose job it is to govern whom . . .'

'Dude,' I go, 'I've actually got to be at the hospital in, like, ten minutes?'

'They gave spivs like Josh and Kyle what they wanted. Unfettered capital markets. The elevation of the City above all else. And what has it delivered? An economy entirely reliant on a financial sector engaging in riskier and riskier activities. We're all going to end up paying the price for their greed. And their arrogance.'

'Dude,' I make the mistake of going, 'why don't you say all that shit on camera?' and he's suddenly staring into space, lost in thought.

*

The thing is, roysh, I don't know how it can be that I could get to, like, twenty-seven years of age and no one – we're *talking* no one – has ever mentioned the size of the old Shiva, good, bad or indifferent.

But now even Harvey says it belongs on Mount Rushmore and of course I have to crack on then that I know what Mount Rushmore is.

'Okay, what about this one?' I go.

I'm standing side-on to the mirror, holding photographs of various noses up to my face. I've got to pick one and I haven't got long.

Harvey laughs. 'It's a bit, I don't know,' he goes, 'doughy.'

I'm like, 'Doughy?'

'It's, like, a boxer's nose,' he goes, shuffling through the deck. 'Hey, what about this one?' and he hands me one that for some reason makes me think of Reese Witherspoon. I hold it up to my face. He's there, 'That is *such* a good look for you.'

I'm like, 'Are you sure it's not a bit, I don't know, girlie?'

'But you *want* a pretty nose, right?'

'I suppose.'

He hands me another one to try.

I ask him how Hugo is and his face lights up. He says they're going horseback riding this weekend in the Santa Monica Mountains and I tell him I'm delighted for him, which I am, although – and this isn't jealousy – I'm just hoping he's still going to have time for me.

I'm there, 'Remember what I said, Dude, don't settle down too early. Learn a lesson from the master. Live your life.'

'Well,' he goes, 'I phoned Mike.'

'Phoned him? What did you do that for?'

'Just to tell him not to contact me. I've met someone and I'm, like, really happy.'

I've always wondered why people need to tell their exes that. Me, I just drop them like a three-foot putt. End of.

'This one makes me look like a focking Teletubby,' I go.

He laughs and shuffles through the deck again. At the same time, he's there, 'Hey, I can't wait to meet your sister.'

'Fock,' I go. 'I almost forgot *she* was coming.'

'But you're happy she's coming, right?'

I tell him it's complicated and he asks me how complicated.

I'm there, 'Well, before we were brother and sister, we actually had . . .'

'History?'

'Well, I was going to say intercourse – but history, yeah.'

His jaw just drops.

This one makes me look like the focking Grinch.

'You're the first person I've actually discussed this with,' I go, 'aport from my best friend. And a bunch of total strangers in addiction counselling.'

He's still in shock.

'In fairness,' I go. 'You've got to see this girl – even you'd be into her.'

'Even *me*?' he goes. He laughs. 'You mean *she* could be the one to cure me of this terrible affliction?'

'You know what I mean,' I go. 'And the whole reason I didn't want her coming over here is that I'm scared that my feelings for her won't have changed.'

'Hey, don't beat yourself up,' he goes, which is exactly what I need to hear, roysh, because I *can* be a bit hord on myself sometimes? 'You said it yourself – you didn't know she was your sister when you had . . . relations. Your feelings for her will resolve themselves – but not until you spend time around her.'

He's actually wise beyond his years, this dude.

I'm there, 'It's just, I don't want to end up feeling like some sexual deviant – even though we're only, like, *half*-brother and sister?'

'And cut!' Johnny Sarno goes, then he storts giving us, like, a round of applause with, like, the usual big smile on his face. The rest of the crew join in then. Apparently, we've, like, nailed the scene, although I'm not a hundred per cent happy with it.

'Johnny,' I go, 'I wouldn't mind reshooting that again. See, the whole thing about the nose job is it's *not* supposed to be for, like, cosmetic reasons? It's supposed to be because I'm having breathing difficulties from a kick in the boat I got back in the glory days . . .'

'We'll handle it in the editing suite,' he goes, without even looking at me.

I'm there, 'I think I'd prefer . . .' but he just, like, cuts me off.

'This isn't the movies,' he goes. 'We've got thirty minutes of television to film every week. We're already behind schedule,' and then he shouts, 'Can we get that doctor in here?'

Johnny tells me to put on my hospital gown and get into bed, which I automatically do.

I cop San – as in San Sancilio – standing just behind the camera, checking himself out in one of the monitors, like the crazy fock that he is.

'Okay,' Johnny shouts, 'you know how this works – same as before. No lines, no script and forget about the cameras. San, you walk in. Ross, you show him the nose you picked. San, you go through the procedure with him. Ross, you talk about maybe one or two concerns you have. San, you quote him some of those statistics you told me about success and failure rates . . .'

I'm like, 'Failure rates? Whoa back!'

'And . . . action!'

San walks in. 'Hello, Ross.'

It feels like a scene from, like, *Days of Our Lives?*

I'm there, 'Er, yeah, hi . . .'

'Haff you chosen a noss thet you would like?'

I hum and haw for a little bit, then I hand him the one that
Harvey thought looked amazing on me. Out of the corner
of my eye, I can see that Harvey's delighted.

'Aha!' San goes. 'Reese Weeterspun!'

'Is it, like, *actually* Reese Witherspoon's?'

'Yes! Thees wheel look ferry nice on your fess.'

'Well,' I go, throwing a sly look to the camera, 'it's not
about how it looks – it's as long as I can breathe again. God,
if I could get my hands on that Gonzaga number eight!'

'Stop talking to the camera!' Johnny shouts. 'San, continue.'

'Ferry goot,' he goes. 'First, I wheel giff to you a general
anaesthetic, which means gutenight, yes? Sleeeepy byebyes.
Then, I wheel cut you here, here and here. You feel nahthing.
Then, I wheel chop away all of thees bone and cartilage . . .'

I'm there, 'Okay, I don't know if you remember what happened last time – best if you don't give me the details.'

He's there, 'Ferry goot. But I giff to you a noss like Elle
Woods, yes? *Don't stomp your leetle last seesun Prada shoes at me,
honey. Excuse me, thees are not last seesun shoes.* Clessic, clessic
comedy, yes?'

'If you're into that kind of shit.'

'*It hess come to my attention thet the maintenance staff ees sweetch-
ing our toilet paypare from Charmeen to generic. All those who are
opposed to chafing, please say aye.*'

He laughs like it's the funniest thing he's ever heard.

I'm there, 'Er, just getting back to the whole operation thing?
Like I said, as long as I can actually breathe properly . . .'

'Yes,' he goes. 'And you wheel look ferry pretty. And do
not be nerfous. I haff done thees many times. Many, many

happy endings. But sometimes, I haff to say to you, if too much of the old noss is cut away, then the breedge wheel collapse and you wheel be deformed. Boo-hoo, ferry sad.'

'What?'

'Also, I say to you, if the teep of the noss is over-rotated, your nostreels wheel look like apeeg.'

'Apeeg?'

'Oink, oink, yes?'

'Jesus Christ!'

'No woman in the world like a men who look like apeeg, no?'

I'm suddenly having second thoughts again.

'For the stateestics, this happen in only eight per cent of my cases.'

I'm there, 'Eight per cent? Er, you know what? I think I'm going take two or three days to have another think about this.'

'You cannot,' he goes. 'Tomorrow I am – how to say? – deporteed.'

'Did you say deported?'

'Deporteed back to Ecuador. Say gutebye to Hollywood, say gutebye my bebby. Beely Joll. Ferry sad. Ferry sad to leave before I can fess my accusers on the Feetness to Precteese Committee.'

I'm like, 'Fitness to practice?' and I automatically throw back the sheets.

Trevion all of a sudden appears. 'Put him out!' he shouts. 'Put him out!' and two nurses appear out of nowhere, roysh, and hold me down while San grabs, like, a huge syringe, squeezes the air out of the top of it, then jabs it into my orm.

My eyes get suddenly heavy. The last thing I hear is Harvey go, 'Oh! My! God!' and Trevion go, 'Goodnight, Joycie!'

I'm like, 'Just don't make me look like . . .' and I'm out of the game before I can even *say* La Toya Jackson.

'Let me tell you,' Trevion goes, 'you're pretty as a fucking girl under them bandages.'

He's driving and I'm sitting in the passenger seat, still groggy. I'm there, 'I can't believe what you did.'

I'm in agony – and we're talking total agony.

'You're a total orsehole,' I go, because he got San to do the focking lot – the lipo, the abdominal resculpt, the pectoral implants, the new calves and the rhinoplasty, obviously.

'Yeah, you betcha,' he goes. 'Pretty as a fucking girl.'

I check myself out in the mirror on the back of the sun visor. I've got two humungous black eyes and I've been told I'm going to have to breathe through my mouth for the next week. I'm a family allowance book away from being an actual skobie.

'And, let me tell *you*,' he goes, 'poor San was *crying* at the airport this morning? Yeah, crying like a fucking baby. And it wasn't because the Feds escorted him onto the plane neither. No, no, no. They were tears of fucking happiness, my friend. That's right. Kept saying how pretty your nose was. I says to him, "What a way to go, San! What a way to go!"'

I shake my head, which even hurts. 'Giving someone plastic surgery against their will,' I go. 'I'm not surprised they deported him.'

'Well, it was more *extradited*,' he goes. 'Tomato, tomayto. But, hey, he wants pictures, the works. I got a hotmail address for his attorney.'

My nose, by the way, like my whole body, is totally bandaged up. 'So how long do I have to leave these on for?' I go, still majorly pissed off here.

'Three, four weeks minimum,' he goes. 'The nose, the longer the better. Less chance of collapse.'

'You're saying now there's a chance it's going to collapse?'

'Hey, there's always a chance. It's not a biggie. San says all we got to do is harvest some cartilage from your septum. Failing that, your fucking ear.'

'What?'

'Don't worry, he wrote it all out for me. There's a napkin there in the glove compartment.'

I whip out the napkin and just, like, stare at it. It's all, like, lines and squiggles. 'It's like focking cave drawings,' I go.

He laughs. 'Doctors and their writing, huh? And he *was* in handcuffs, remember.'

'You have got to be focking shitting me!'

'Hey, pipe down, McDreamy. Chances are we won't need it. I got other news. That sister of yours arrived yesterday morning . . .'

'Erika?'

He gives a sort of, like, long wolf-whistle.

I shake my head.

'She's a fucking beauty, ain't she?'

I'm there, 'Don't remind me.'

'A real beauty. And let me tell you, Johnny and the MTV boys are very happy. She got a great work ethic . . .'

Which is hilarious – she's hordly worked a day since she left school. Like the rest of us.

'She comes in, catches two, three hours sleep, then she and Sorcha, they go get a fucking hair soak together. They have lunch in the Spanish Kitchen, then they hit Barneys, shopping for shoes.'

'I've seen them two run *up* a down-escalator to get at focking shoes.'

'Well,' he goes, 'MTV got three fucking hours of footage – usable. Let me tell you, Johnny did some work on *Laguna*

226

and the first season of *The Hills*. He says they're gonna be the new Heidi and LC.'

'I'm sure they'll be happy to hear that.'

'The kids are gonna love them. And that's to say nothing of your mother . . .'

I actually turn and look at him. I don't believe it, but I'm pretty sure I see that scar-laden, mangled face of his blush.

'Good idea,' I go. 'Say nothing.'

He shakes his head, roysh, like he's in awe of her, which of course he is. 'She got a record deal,' he goes.

I'm there, 'A record deal?'

'You fucking bet, a record deal.'

I actually laugh. 'Have you ever *heard* her sing?'

'She's got a beautiful voice. Anyways, they clean all that shit up in the studio. You think Beyoncé can sing?'

'I would have presumed she could, yeah.'

'Beyoncé sounds like two stevedores arguing over a prostitute.'

'Are you serious?'

'Yeah, it's all studio trickery. Anyway, what it is, is Columbia got their hands on some old Jeff Buckley recordings – they were in some schmo's attic. Or that's the *story*. Personally, I think they had them all along but they was never good enough to put out. Good tunes, though. "*Je N'en Connais Pas La Fin*". "Grapefruit Moon". "Please Please Please Let Me Get What I Want". All that shit. So what they want to do is clean them up and get your mother to sing every second verse . . .'

'You've got! To be pulling! My stick!'

'Fyon Hoola O'Carroll-Kelly sings a collection of heart-warming duets with the late but very great Jeff Buckley.'

'And you think *actual* people will buy that?'

'Hey,' he goes, 'people will eat shit if you put enough Splenda on it.'

'I doubt that,' I go. 'I seriously doubt that.'

He's quiet for minute and I know he's, like, building up to something – something I almost definitely *don't* want to hear?

'I think I've fallen in love with her,' he eventually goes.

I'm like, 'Spare me.'

'Sure,' he goes, 'go ahead and laugh. Let me tell *you* something, Chico, I ain't never felt nothing like this before. I thought I was done with all that, see. You spend six months in a prisoner-of-war camp, in the care of men with nothing to do all day except dream up new ways of torturing you, a certain light goes out in your fucking soul, you know what I'm saying?'

I'm there, 'Come back to me after you've known her a month.' Which he ignores.

'Seventy-five,' he goes, 'and I feel like I'm seventeen again . . .'

I think about the old man and Helen. I'm there, 'There's a lot of it about, believe me.'

So we pull into the driveway. Johnny Sarno's waiting outside for us. He opens the door for me, all smiles as usual. Various other people come running, including a make-up bird, who happens to be a ringer for Kim Raver. She's, like, poised with the powder brush.

'Do something to emphasize the bandaging,' Johnny goes.

I'm like, 'Emphasize? Do you not mean . . .' but she storts slapping me with the brush, roysh, before I can even think of the word unemphasize.

'Okay, your motivation for this scene,' Johnny goes, 'is that your sister has come over from Ireland. You haven't seen her since the night you found out she *was* your sister. So you're going to have all sorts of emotions – confusion, probably affection . . .'

He grabs me by the orm of my T-shirt and literally drags

me into the gaff, still smiling, through the hall and down to the door of the kitchen, which is closed. 'Now,' he goes, 'we've got cameras everywhere in there to make sure we capture the magical moment when you two finally come face to face. And don't worry if you fluff it first time – we can always go back and do it again.'

He opens the door, roysh, just wide enough to stick his head through. 'Yes, he's here,' I hear him go. 'Are we all set?'

Then he goes, 'You girls act like you're having just one of your everyday conversations,' and then he closes over the door again.

'And . . . *action*!' he shouts, then he sort of, like, indicates the door handle to me.

I'm actually kacking it. I don't know what her reaction's going to be. But I take, like, a deep breath, then I go in.

'Did you *see* the butler-inspired Zac Posen that Naomi Watts wore to the LA premiere of *The Painted Veil*?' Sorcha's going, and it has to be said she's a natural. I suppose she's wanted to be famous all her life.

They're both standing with their backs to me, at the Nespresso. 'It's like, when bad clothes happen to good people!'

'Hey,' I go.

They suddenly both turn around.

It's like, fock! Erika looks incredible – whatever a hair soak is. We both just stare at each other for what seems like forever? Then all of a sudden she comes chorging across the kitchen towards me, throws her orms around me and bursts into, basically, tears. The number of times I've seen her cry you could count twice on the fingers of one hand.

'Oh, Ross!' she keeps giving it. 'Oh, Ross!' and I realize then, roysh, that I'm actually crying, too.

'I'm sorry,' I end up going. 'I needed space. I just didn't know how to handle the whole situation.'

She smells of buttermilk and *Agent Provocateur*.

'We're *both* still in shock,' she goes. 'But you're my brother, Ross. And I'm your sister . . .'

I can feel the soft skin of her cheek against mine.

'I know,' I go, realizing at that exact moment . . .

. . . with total horror, I hope I don't *need* to add . . .

. . . that I've an oar on me that could row the whole focking lot of us to Hawaii.

'Half-sister,' I think about going, but in the end I don't, knowing that I have to act fast here. It's not only her who might notice – there's seven focking cameras in the room waiting to put this out to a worldwide audience of, like, hundreds of billions of people.

So I end up just looking her in the eye and going, 'I think what we probably both need is to sit down,' and I sort of, like, turn my body away from her – like I'm evading a tackle in rugby – and I plonk my orse down on one of Sorcha's high stools, thinking, no one ever notices you've a stiffy when you're sitting down.

She sits down on the stool beside me. My hand is on the black morble countertop and she lays hers on top of mine and sort of, like, strokes it with her thumb.

Which obviously *doesn't* help?

She goes, 'I'm looking forward to us getting to know each other.'

I look at Sorcha and notice that she's crying as well.

I've never known Erika to be anything other than a bitch. This whole scene is, like, too weird for words. 'You've only ever been a wagon to me,' I go, which must be true, roysh, because *she* even laughs?

She's there, 'Well, you've always made it difficult for people to like you,' which is possibly also true – though there's a lot *would* disagree.

'But this is a chance,' she goes, 'for us to start all over again. I always wanted a brother.'

I'm there, 'I suppose I always wanted a sister.'

'Okay, beautiful,' Johnny shouts. 'Now, move on. Sorcha, ask her about her mother.'

'By the way, Erika, how are things with, like, your mum?' Sorcha goes.

Erika shakes her head. 'I swear to God, Sorcha – I never, ever want to see her again.'

I'm pretty sure that Sorcha *knows* the full Jack by now, but she does a good job of cracking on *not* to? 'Oh my God,' she goes, with the full drama. Like an old pro. 'Why?'

I always forget she played Phoebe Meryll in the Rathmines and Rathgar Musical Society's production of *The Yeomen of the Guard* when she was only, like, fifteen.

I'm there, 'Why do you think? Imagine, after all those years, finding out that *he's* your old man. No offence, Erika, but what the fock was your mother thinking?'

She jumps straight to his defence, of course. 'Ross, he's doing his best to make up for lost time,' she goes. 'He really wants to be a father to me.'

'Well, that's going to be weird,' I go. 'Especially with them being back together, which I still can't believe, by the way. You know they were spotted coming out of the Bedroom Studio? Middle of Dalkey Main Street?'

Sorcha turns around to Erika and goes, 'Do you not think you're being a bit hard on *her*, though? Keeping it quiet required more than one person's silence, remember.'

'Look,' Erika goes, 'I'm entitled to be angry with her. You *know* how close I was to my mum, Sorcha.'

'That's why I'm saying it. You were like me and *my* mum? As in, Best *Best* Friends?'

'How could she keep something like that from me, then?

When I was a little girl, she always said to me, let's not have any secrets from each other.'

'There's secrets and there's secrets,' I go. 'But getting knocked up by my old man's not something you'd be shouting from the rooftops.'

'And cut!' Johnny shouts. 'Okay, Ross, I need you out of the kitchen. Girls, I want to reshoot the scene where you're waiting for him to arrive . . .'

I look at Erika. I'm like, 'It's good to see you.'

She smiles at me and squeezes my hand. 'It'll be easier to talk when it's not all . . . this,' she goes and she flicks her head in the direction of the studio lights, which have us all sweating focking bricks here.

'Sorcha, I loved the Naomi Watts line,' Johnny goes, studying his clipboard, 'but can you mention being happy with the Narciso Rodriguez black strappy sheath you bought earlier, because they've given us one for you to wear in a future scene . . .'

I jump down off the stool, totally forgetting that I'm still in, like, battle mode.

'And one of you,' he goes, 'I don't care which – say that you can't wait to check out Michael Katz on *Burton Way* . . .'

The next thing I hear is Erika go, 'Ross?' then Sorcha go, 'Oh! My God!' and they both put their hands up to their faces and I realize, roysh, that they're both staring at the enormous – and I *mean* enormous – bulge in my trousers.

He answers on the fourth ring. He's all, 'Hello,' and of course I'm not going to give him the pleasure of saying it back to him.

I'm just there, 'I hear you're back with Erika's old dear – as in *with* with?'

'Clearly nothing wrong with the transatlantic grapevine,' he goes, 'quote-unquote,' like he's not even ashamed of it.

I'm there, 'What are you, a focking teenager?'

He actually thinks it's funny. 'You know, I almost feel like I am. Helen here's got me trying all sorts of crazy things. Last night she took me to Eddie Rockers . . .'

'It's Eddie *Rockets*,' I go. 'And I can't believe you went there. I've been going there for focking years.'

'Then she has me listening to – what's her name, Helen? Oh, yes, Rhianna. Well, there's even talk of me getting one of these *iPods*. Have you ever heard the like of it, Ross?'

'Er, *no*? I focking haven't. Wait a minute – are you two in, like, bed there?'

'Of course,' he goes. 'It's after midnight. What time is it stateside?'

'Whoa back, horsy! You're in bed together?'

'Ross, we're in love.'

'You're not in love. *She's* desperate and *you* can't believe your luck that anyone would focking want you. And you're both making a show of yourselves. Have you no shame?'

He's there, 'What's wrong with your voice, Kicker?' trying to change the subject.

'What do you mean, what's wrong with my voice? I had a focking nose job.'

'A nose job? Why?'

'Er, maybe because I didn't want to grow old looking like you. *And* we're making a reality TV show, if you must know.'

'Oh,' he just goes and it's obvious he hasn't a focking clue what I'm talking about.

In the background, I can hear Helen telling him to ask me about Erika.

'Oh, yes,' he goes, 'you haven't heard from Erika, have you?'

I'm like, 'No – why would I have heard from her?'

'It's just, as you well know, she and her mother had words – words with a capital W. A lot of things said. Heat of the moment and so forth. But she's checked out of the Merrion and we're both worried about her . . .'

'Maybe she killed herself because she couldn't live with being related to you.'

'No, she hasn't done anything so drastic, thank God. No, I had a text from her yesterday, saying she's fine. She just won't tell us where she is.'

'Have you not thought that maybe she needs some space? No, because the two of you are too busy with your focking *High School Musical* routine.'

I tell him he's a disgrace and I hang up on him.

Harvey arrives back from the jacks – we're sitting outside Swinger's on Beverly, the sun beating down on our faces, the whole bit – and he catches, like, the tail-end of the conversation.

'Was that your *father*?' he goes, like he can't believe anyone could speak to their old man like that. I tell him not to worry, he's actually a penis. And he's used to it. If I was nice to him, it'd be too much of a shock to the system. He'd have a hort attack. Harvey *seems* to understand.

Our Ahi sandwiches arrive.

I ask him how the big romance is going. That's one of the other things I love about myself since I came out here – I've become, like, an amazing conversationalist? He tells me that Hugo's a yoga instructor and that the sex is amazing and at the top of my voice I'm going, 'TMI, Dude! TMI!'

He laughs, then he says it's not just the things they do together. They talk – as in really talk. And Hugo listens to him.

'I listen to you as well,' I hear myself go. I don't *know* why? But it's actually nice when he says he knows I listen.

'Mike never did,' he goes. 'He was, like, all about his Maserati and his time at Brown and how his wife was such a good person and if she wasn't, how come she ended up teaching children with special needs?'

I touch my bandaged nose, thinking I probably shouldn't spend too long outside. I don't want to end up with, like, tan lines on my face. 'So,' I go, 'have you had another think about this whole TV thing?'

See, he's changed his mind about appearing in *Ross, His Mother, His Wife and Her Lover* and now he won't sign the release form for the footage of the two of us in the hospital, where I'm trying on various noses. Which means, roysh, that MTV are going to have to either drop that entire scene or somehow splice Harvey out of it.

He says he's just not ready for something like this. Of course, if that's his decision, roysh, it'd be unfair to, like, push him.

'I'm disappointed,' I go. 'But I'll get over it.'

He looks suddenly sad. I'm wondering is he going to eat those potato chips.

'Look, can I tell you something?' he goes.

I'm there, 'Of course you can. Fock's sake, Harve.'

He takes, like, a deep breath. 'Remember before, when you asked how my parents took the news?'

'Yeah.'

I take a potato chip. Fock, my abs and pecs are sore today.

'They don't know, Ross. They don't know that I'm gay.'

I'm there, 'Fock! But the thing about reality TV is, you can be whoever you want to be. No one's saying you have to do gay shit. You can be in it as just some random mate of mine.'

He shakes his head. 'You don't understand,' he goes. 'They know nothing about my LA life.'

'Your LA life? What are you talking about?'

'Ross, when I'm here, I can be me. When I'm at home . . .'

'What?'

'I'm different. Look, I grew up in this macho family. I've got, like, five brothers. They tinker with cars. They like sports. You understand?'

'Er, I think so.'

'When I call home, I put on this, like, deep voice. I read the football pages so I can pretend to know what my father's talking about. They don't even know what I do here. They think I'm in college.'

I'm there, 'Dude, you have to tell them – take it from someone who always calls it like it is. With *my* old pair, I'm always thinking, you know, what if something happens to them and there ends up being things I haven't said to them? That's why you hear me offloading to my old man like that. I do it to *her* as well. You can't live with regrets.'

He doesn't say anything, roysh, except that I should maybe get in out of the sun – otherwise I'm going to end up with, like, a rhino tan.

Er, *remind* me again why we're here?

I'm actually talking about Whole Foods in Santa Monica, but Sorcha looks at me like I've just shed a load in one of her Roberto Cavallis.

'Because,' she goes, '*some* of us don't want to see our children poisoned by Agri-Business,' then she turns around to Erika and says that there's no point in even trying to talk to me because I've no even interest in, like, sustainability.

It's all for the benefit of the cameras, of course.

Erika gives me a little smile and sort of, like, rolls her eyes, as if to say, she's a bit focking much, isn't she? And it's amazing, roysh, because it's suddenly, like, brother and sister sharing an actual joke?

She looks amazing as well in, like, the Pencey mini and Alice + Olivia strappy top that I let her put on my credit cord this morning because her luggage is actually lost. I tell her I was talking to the old man earlier and she looks suddenly worried.

She's there, 'You didn't tell him I'm here, did you?' and I tell her no, there's no way in the world I'd do that. I'd rather let the focker sweat.

She takes Honor from me. I suppose she's, like, *her* auntie now as well.

We're in the artisan bread section, where Sorcha is, like, squeezing various loaves, testing them for what she calls *give*. 'Jackie Keller, the nutritionist who works with Ginnifer Goodwin, said somewhere that it's possible to *eat* a good proportion of your recommended daily water intake and artisan breads are, like, seventy-five per cent moisture?'

Me and Erika pull faces like we actually care.

Then we get back to, like, family matters. 'Erika, I know you hate your old dear,' I go. 'But can I make a case for you hating *him* just as much – possibly even more?'

She's there, 'Ross, Charles hasn't *been* in my life? The point is, *she* has? She had, like, twenty-seven years to tell me the truth – but that would have been, oh, too inconvenient for her.'

I'm there, 'Would you not think of even texting her? She's going to need all the support she can get if she's got herself mixed up with him again,' but there's, like, too much anger in her for her to see sense at the moment.

Sorcha pushes the trolley on. She says she saw Ashley Tisdale and Jared Murillo in here and that was, like, two weeks before she got a text alert to say they were even dating?

I grab a leaflet on the shop's policy regording genetically modified food and make, like, a paper airplane, which I then throw. I get unbelievable distance from it as well. Honor just, like, squeals with excitement and even Erika seems pretty impressed.

We head for the checkout and the bird – not the Rory Best, it has to be said – storts ringing our shit through. Organic vanilla ricemilk. Grain-fed chicken. Rennet- and rBST-free cheddar. Chewy Multivitamin Gummy Fruits. It's like, porty time at our place!

I stort packing all the shit into a biodegradable paper bag.

Sorcha picks up a copy of *Us Weekly* while she's waiting to hear the damage and mentions that waist-cinching dresses are going to be *so* in this year, although she'd almost literally kill for the tea-length vintage Ossie Clark that Keira Knightley wore to the Oscar nominee luncheon.

I'm actually putting the flaxseed oil in the bag when, for some reason, I happen to look up and, out of the corner of my eye, I notice the cover of *People* magazine. Or, more specifically, a photograph of me leaving Barney's Beanery two nights ago with a bird called Shelby Pienkowski, another of Trevion's up-and-coming actresses.

The headline is like, 'From No Job to Nose Job', and then underneath it's like, 'But Socialite O'Carroll-Kelly Keeps New Schnoz Under Wraps!'

My hands are, like, shaking with anger, to the point where I find it difficult to even turn to pages fourteen, fifteen, sixteen and seventeen, not to mention the 'Week to Forget For' feature on thirty-five, which I also made it into.

The main story's like, 'Celebrity wannabe Ross O'Carroll-Kelly has always had a nose for controversy. Remember giving espresso to a minor? Remember being thrown off the set of a Disney movie? Now, the wild child of literary sensation Fionnuala O'Carroll-Kelly is looking to reinvent himself – with a brand *new* nose!' and there's not a focking mention of me getting kicked in the face against Gonzaga.

'O'Carroll-Kelly (27) was spotted leaving a West Hollywood bar with promising actress Shelby Pienkowski (*One Tree Hill* pilot, *Angel* pilot, *My So-Called Life* pilot) late on Saturday night, sporting two black eyes and with his nose heavily strapped.'

Sorcha, who's, like, reading over my shoulder, goes, 'Oh my God, Ross, you are turning into *such* a male slut.'

I'm like, 'Sorcha, it's a set-up. Johnny Sarno just wanted a few shots of me out and about with some random bird, doing my thing. Give the public a taste of what I'm like.'

The story continues, 'The pair were later seen at nearby Coco de Ville, grabbing a table with *Hills* stars Audrina Partridge, Frankie Delgado and Doug Reinhardt,' which is total horseshit, by the way. 'Eventually, the group moved to the dancefloor, forming a circle and dancing to songs like Justin Timberlake's "Rock Your Body" and Madonna's "Holiday". "Ross looked a bit like Hannibal Lecter with all that strapping on his face," said one onlooker. "But he didn't seem self-conscious at all."

'Shelby wore a gold sequinned bubble mini dress by Jovani with Rene Caovilla sandals.

'A spokesman for the Irish lothario – who is separated from his wife Sorcha (meaning 'fair one') – refused to comment. However, a friend confirmed that he decided to have the surgery after years of jibes about his formerly wide and misshapen nose.'

I'm there, 'Bastard!'

'It's even rumoured that it was his monster schnozzle that came between him and former beau Lauren Conrad. What she'll think of the new one is anyone's guess. The friend said that Ross has been told to keep it under wraps for at least four weeks.'

I end up flipping the lid. I whip out my phone and ring

Trevion. 'You focker!' are the first words out of my mouth. 'You've stitched me up. Again.'

He's there, 'Hey, pipe down, Tin Strawn.'

'Coco de Ville?' I go. 'Frankie Delgado? This story's got your pawprints all over it, so don't even think about denying it.'

He's there, 'Hey, I'm keeping your name in the papers, aren't I? How about some gratitude?'

'Gratitude? The deal was we were going to say it was, like, a rugby injury.'

I get, like, a stabbing pain in my chest. I should stop shouting or I'll burst my stitches.

'You think anyone's interested,' he goes, 'in some sportsman-who-never-was, having an operation to help him breathe better? You know what people want?'

'What?'

'They want to know that the stars they see on TV are every bit as vain and unhappy with themselves as they are.'

'Oh, is that what you think?'

'Yes, it fucking is, Dorothy. People are going to tune in in their tens of millions to see you take them bandages off your nose. Now quit whining. I got news. Johnny's over the fucking moon with the footage he's got so far . . .'

I'm there, 'He's not going to use the bit where . . .'

He's like, 'The bit where you get an erection in your pants sitting next to your fucking sister? No. Even MTV's got standards. But the pilot's going out second Sunday in May . . .'

I'm like, 'Whoa!'

'Which means we got to keep working. You see that wife and that sister of yours, you tell them they're having breakfast in Viktor's tomorrow – just two broads having a girlie chat. As for you, your mother's in the recording studio eleven o'clock in the morning . . .'

'Mariah Carey,' I go. In other words, I'll be there.

'By the way,' he goes, 'I'm thinking about telling her how I feel.'

I laugh. I actually laugh.

'What,' he goes, 'you think I'm too old for her? Too ugly? Is it these scars?'

I'm just there, 'Look, just don't say I didn't warn you.'

I ring Christian, just to let him know that his best friend in the world is about to become a huge stor on MTV. It goes straight to his voicemail, so I leave a message telling him that I have news – we're talking major news – but he doesn't even ring me back.

'You like fah-ing terrapins?'

I turn around. There's a dude standing there with, like, long hair and big aviator shades. Must be 'Fah-ing' Ronnie Wheen – as in the dude who's producing this so-called record?

I'm there, 'I have to say I've never given them much thought,' then we end up both staring into this massive tank in the corner of the studio. They *are* pretty cool, I suppose – they've even got their own little Hollywood sign in there.

'They're my passion,' Ronnie goes. I probably should mention that he's, like, English? 'You wanna see my 'ouse – they're fah-ing everywhere. See this little fella, keeps eeself to eeself? That's Syd. You know his song, "Terrapin"? Course you do. Poor fah-ing Syd. Breaks my fah-ing 'eart to see him today. All that fah-ing talent . . .'

I obviously haven't a fah-ing bog what he's banging on about.

He's there, 'So this Finnhooler's your mum, eh?'

I'm like, 'Yeah – worse luck.'

'Nah,' he goes, 'she got a fah-ing great voice.'

241

I'm there, 'There must be something wrong with your ears, then. She sounds like a pensioner bending down for the TV remote.'

Ronnie shakes his head like he couldn't *actually* agree less? 'I've worked wiv the best and she's fah-ing up there. The uvver fing is, this idea's the perfect fah-ing synergy, in'it? They make a TV programme of 'er recording an owbum – the show promotes the fah-ing record and the record promotes the fah-ing show. Everyone's 'appy – way of the fah-ing future.'

I turn around to the console and I'm suddenly staring at the old dear through the window of the sound booth, thinking, What! The fock! Is she wearing?

This isn't horseshit, roysh, she's got on, like, a babydoll dress with leopardskin ballet flats and – sweet suffering fock – her hair up in a beehive, like Amy focking Winehouse. It would actually be hilarious if it wasn't so sad.

Trevion arrives with Johnny Sarno in tow. The way *he* reacts, you'd swear he just walked in to find Megan Fox sniffing his boxers.

'Look at you!' he goes, his big pumice-stone face going red. She gives him a little girlie wave through the glass – nothing for me, of course. Trevion turns around to Johnny. 'You give him his instructions yet?'

Johnny looks at me – everything seems to be funny to this dude – and goes, 'What we want from you is exactly what you did in Book Soup. Remember, you're going to be the Spencer Pratt character. So she's going to start singing and you need to go in there and start verbally haranguing her. Do you think you can do that?'

'Dude,' I go, 'this isn't even work for me.'

Trevion's there, 'We need to do it quickly, too. Then we're going to get you out of here, because your mother's got a

Of course, after half an hour of nagging from the two of them, I put mine on, but then I went and wrote the word 'Yourself' underneath, which *is* funny, you'd have to admit.

'Acclaimed author, singer and the undoubted star of MTV's *Ross, His Mother, His Wife and Her Lover*, ladies and gentlemen, wearing classic Miu Miu patent heels, let's give a good old-fashioned – let me see can I say this right – *caid milla failty* to the beautiful Irish *coleen*, Fionnuala O'Carroll-Kelly!'

She ends up getting the biggest cheer of any of them. This country's taste is seriously up its hole.

Her face suddenly comes up on the huge screen they've got and I'm staring at her big, all of a sudden bee-stung lips and it's like, *who* gets botoxed before something like this? She looks like a focking monkey with hot tea in its mouth.

The race, I probably should say, is a straight hundred-metre dash, the length of the running track. But before it actually storts, roysh, there ends up being a major borney over whether Nicolette Sheridan's wedge sandals are a technical breach of the rules. Alison Sweeney and Lisa Rinna are of the strong opinion that, even though they're high, they're not actual heels? Tinsley Mortimer – while accepting that they meet the minimum four-inch height requirement – argues that she was told stilettos and that wedges give Nicolette an unfair advantage over the rest of the, I don't know, grid.

While this argument is raging, I should point out, the old dear is staying out of it, with Trevion in her ear, telling her to concentrate on her own race and no doubt bulling her up as well. She's doing all these supposed stretching exercises, though take it from someone who played sport at the highest level, she hasn't a bog what she's doing.

After, like, five full minutes of arguing, the judges decide that wedge sandals, while possibly against the spirit of the rules, do not represent a material breach and Nicolette Sheridan should be allowed to race.

Then, at last, it's, like, game time.

Trevion kisses the old dear on the lips and I watch her mouth the words I love you, then he says it back to her, like the saps that they are.

'Take your mark,' the announcer suddenly goes. He's like, 'Set . . .' and then, after a few seconds, there's a bang and they're away. *She's* first out of the blocks – *has* to be the centre of attention, of course – and she straight away puts a good five yords between her and Alison Sweeney in second, with Tinsley Mortimer a close third and the other two – it has to be said – nowhere

After all the hassle, Nicolette Sheridan looks immediately out of the race after a strap opens, one of her sandals goes flying and she ends up having to go back to, like, put it on again. 'Oh my God,' Sorcha says excitedly. 'I was going to say that when the others were trying to get her to change into those Zanottis. Wedge sandals are really light, but – oh my God – they *always* open when you try to run in them.'

The old dear's, like, ten yords ahead and moving like a focking train. Sorcha's like, 'I can see now where you got it from, Ross,' and what she obviously means is my turn of pace, roysh, but there's no way I'm going to let her associate me with her.

'I'd beat her running constipated,' I make sure to go.

Erika's going, 'Come on, Fionnuala! Come on, Fionnuala!' like the kind of knicker-wetting girls she absolutely hated at school, then she's at Honor, telling her to cheer for her grandmother.

Honor just goes, '*Hen hao! Hen hao! Hen hao!*' leaving it open as to who she's actually up *for* here?

The old dear stretches her legs and suddenly she's, like, fifteen yords ahead. I'm standing there thinking, superglue or no superglue, there's no way it can hold that shoe together for much longer, espcially given *her* weight.

By the time she reaches the fifty-metre mork, she's already dropped Tinsley Mortimer and, in fairness to her, Alison Sweeney is the only one making an actual race out of it. But even she's way behind now.

'They're actually *my* Miu Mius,' Sorcha is telling people in the crowd, obviously excited. 'They *are* actual high-heels? But they *feel* like flats.'

Nicolette Sheridan loses a sandal again, the other one this time, and all the women in the crowd exchange what would have to be described as knowing looks.

The old dear is, like, twenty yords from the line and the crowd is going ballistic. 'Go on!' they're giving it. 'Go on!'

Ten yords from the line, I'm thinking, why didn't I use, like, ordinary glue?

Then it happens. And, I have to say, it takes even me by surprise.

What I see first is her orms sort of, like, flailing, if that's the word? They certainly go up in the air and her body sort of, like, lists to the left, to use the old *Titanic*, I suppose, ter-minology. She runs on another few steps, roysh, but then her ankle just buckles and she goes down like focking Tupac, literally inches from the line.

I can even see the heel on the track, snapped off, about five metres behind where she's suddenly lying, holding her left ankle and moaning, looking for sympathy basically.

Sorcha screams, though I imagine more for her shoes than for my old dear. Erika looks pretty upset as well.

What happens next, I like to think, is a lesson in what basic-ally separates life's biggest winners from life's biggest losers.

321

Alison Sweeney's hands go up to her face and she runs immediately over to where the old dear's writhing around, to see if she's okay. Tinsley Mortimer and Lisa Rinna forget about the race as well and go to check on her, their faces full of concern.

Nicolette Sheridan, possibly thinking, 'Okay, what would Edie Britt do in this situation?' sees her chance and makes a bolt for the finish line, literally hurdling over the old dear, who fell into her lane, before dipping over the line.

The crowd, it has to be said, are not happy rabbits. In fact, I'm the only one who's actually cheering, obviously having been a bit of a villain myself back in my Senior Cup days. I'm wolf-whistling her and everything as she whips off her Tony Burch wedge sandals and holds them up over her head, basic- ally taunting the crowd with them.

I'm actually gesturing for her to throw them to me when Sorcha goes, 'Ross!' and she says it in a way that means, go and see if your mother's okay?

I throw my eyes up to heaven, then tip over. She's fine, of course. She's got plenty of attention, as in Trevion's, like, crad- ling her head, telling her there's an ambulance on its way, even though she's already said it's only a sprain, and the others are all cooing over her as well.

Then Sorcha and Erika arrive and stort giving her all the sympathy she's looking for.

I end up getting into a bit of a row with this bird who expresses the opinion that the race should be declared void, since everybody knows that Fionnuala is the *real* winner, and I point out, reasonably, that that's not what the record books will show.

It's just as she's calling me a jerk that it happens.

Trevion goes, 'I was going to do this tonight, Fyon Hoola. I was going to take you out to dinner, somewhere real nice –

Ortolan – have the sommelier bring your favourite champagne . . . But you know what? Here's as good a place as any.'

He reaches into his inside pocket and whips out this little black box. Of course, he doesn't even need to open it for me to know what it is. He goes, 'I got a hunk of ice here, Fyon Hoola, says I want to spend the rest of my life with you.'

I'm there, 'Trevion, don't be a focking dope.'

It's a six-carat canary focking diamond.

Sorcha goes, 'Oh! My God!' In fact, everyone goes, 'Oh! My God!' now that I think about it.

He's like, 'What do you say? Will you marry me?'

She stares at *me*, roysh, while she thinks about it, then she turns to him and she goes, 'Yes,' like what she's *actually* being offered is a look at the focking dessert menu. 'I rather think I will.'

9. The dreaming days when the mess was made

I leave a message on Harvey's phone. I'm not sure if the word is, like, garbled? But I tell him that I'm about to get all the bandaging off and that it feels, I don't know, weird him not being here to see the new bod, but especially the new nose, seeing as he was the one who picked it.

I don't go as far as to say that I miss him, blahdy blahdy blah, although that *is* the general vibe?

The nurse sticks her head around the door and asks me if I'm ready yet. I carry on staring at my phone and she goes, 'You know, it's *been* two hours – I don't think she's coming.'

I'm like, '*He*,' and she's there, 'Oh,' and I'm about to tell her that I don't mean it in, you know, *that* way. But I don't.

I stand up. Deep down, I know she's right. I follow her into the little room.

'What I can do,' she goes, 'is just cut the Band-Aids holding the bandages to your face and body, then leave you on your own.'

I'm there, 'Why?'

'A lot of people who have procedures like to see the results in their own time,' and it's only then, roysh, that I realize how *actually* nervous I am?

I whip off my T-shirt anyway and she takes, like, a scissors and cuts the plasters on one side, then sort of, like, smiles at me, as if to say, this is the moment of truth. She looks a bit like America Ferrera looks in *real* life?

'Take your time,' she goes, then she disappears out of the room. I turn around, looking for a mirror. There's one across the room – above, like, a washbasin? – and I tip over to it and stare hord at my reflection. I'm thinking, I could literally look like anything under here.

I'm thinking, okay, here goes.

I grab the corner of the bandage stuck to my upper chest and I close my eyes and give it, like, a shorp tug. It takes off pretty much all of my chest hair.

'Aaaggghhh!' I end up going.

Without opening my eyes, I grab the corner of the bandage covering my pecs and rip it off in the same way, quick and shorp. Then I take, like, a couple of steps backwards and open my eyes.

My jaw pretty much hits the floor. I'm a focking Adonis – and that's not, like, an exaggeration?

Being honest, roysh, I've never looked in the mirror and *not* liked what I've seen? But this is, like, different. I can't actually take my eyes off myself.

Fair focks to San Sancilio – you could zest lemons on my abs and my pecs are like actual tits.

Then I'm looking at my face, thinking, okay, the old Shiva Rose is next. I'm suddenly kacking it again. My face is my fortune, after all, and I'm thinking, what if it's a mess, a real focking chewed toffee of an effort? Would I have to go looking for San Sancilio? Where even *is* Ecuador? And would the VHI even cover me there – if it's, like, Plan E Options?

Then it comes into my head that, as usual, I'm probably *over*-thinking here? I decide to just be brave. The quicker you do it, the better, a bit like ripping off a . . .

I close my eyes, grip the bandage by one corner and just pull. Then, very slowly, I open my eyes again. And I'm left suddenly staring at San's handiwork.

I'm thinking, Fock! *What* has he done to me?

It's magnificent – and that's not a word I'd ever use.

It's possibly the most perfect nose I've ever seen. It makes me look a good twenty per cent better-looking, if you can believe that's even possible. I'm trying to be objective here, but I'm quite honestly one of the best-looking men I've ever seen, although, really, I'd have to leave that for others to say.

Even twenty minutes later, roysh, when I'm heading back to the gaff, I end up nearly hitting a concrete bollard on the freeway because I keep looking at *it* instead of the actual road in front of me. I've got, like, the rearview turned towards me and I can't stop checking it out. Or touching it either.

Those who said that I couldn't get any better-looking have been proven well and truly wrong and naturally I'm thinking, maybe I'll give the old tantric a miss tonight, hit Les Deux instead, or maybe even Goa – have me some non-committal fun. It's literally ages since I've had any. I've got balls like focking planets here and, as I'm pulling into the driveway, it randomly pops into my head that gaseous exchange in plants occurs through pores in the leaves called stomata, the size of which are controlled by guard cells. They open wide in daylight when CO_2 is required for photosynthesis.

I go into the gaff and through the kitchen door I can hear Sorcha mention that Lindsay Lohan has admitted that she's not happy with her weight after her skimpy Shoshanna bikini revealed a much fuller figure at a party at the DKNY Beach House last week.

In my head I'm thinking, yeah? You think *that's* news? Wait'll you get a load of my boat.

I push the door and go in. Sorcha is sitting at the island, flicking through a magazine. The old dear is hobbling around on – get this – crutches, looking for sympathy, like it's something *worse* than a sprain?

They both look up, roysh, at exactly the same time. I go, 'Ta-dahhh!' like a focking magician doing a trick.

I have to say, roysh, I'm not ready for the reaction that I get? Sorcha screams, roysh, and it's a scream that pretty much bursts my eardrums, as in, '*Aaaggghhhh!*'

She looks, it has to be said, terrified, though it's her next line that really throws me. She's there, 'Who *are* you? How did you get in here?'

I look at the old dear, then back at her. I'm there, 'What are you talking about – it's me!'

She goes, 'Just take whatever you want. Don't hurt us. I have a nearly-two-year-old baby.'

I'm there, 'Er, I *know* you've a nearly-two-year-old baby?' and I look at the old dear and I can see that she knows exactly who I am. She goes, 'Don't worry, Sorcha, it's only . . .' but then she stops and I watch her eyes look suddenly over my shoulder.

'It's . . .'

I'm there, 'Go on, tell her . . .'

But then this, like, evil look crosses her face. 'It's some kind of sex fiend,' she shouts. 'Do it, Erika!' and I immediately turn, roysh, to find myself staring not at Erika but down the nozzle of a spray can.

The next thing I hear is, like, a fizzing sound, then I feel the most unbelievable pain in my eyes and I'm straight away blind. I fall to the floor and then they suddenly set upon me – Erika with one of her XOXOs, Sorcha with a rolled-up copy of *Us Weekly*.

I'm lying there going, 'Not the face! Not the face!' and of course it's only when I say that that they realize it's actually me.

Sorcha says that if she was getting married again, it would definitely be, like, a green wedding? As in, all the invites would be on, like, recycled paper, the dress would be made of organic cotton, the food would be sourced locally and, instead of gifts, guests would be asked to donate money to, like, dolphin charities?

Of course, I'm barely even listening to her. I'm just, like, staring at the old dear, going, 'Unbelievable! *Un*-focking-believable!' and what I mean by that is that she spent the morning shopping for a wedding dress, even though she's already married?

And all for the cameras, if you ask me.

She blanks me and asks Erika what she's going to have and Erika says either the *salmone arrostito* or the *zuppa di pesce* and I'm left just shaking my head.

Sorcha says her favourite is definitely the Badgely Mischka – I should point out, we've moved back to dresses now – and the old dear asks whether it made her hips look big, fishing for a compliment.

I tell her that her hips would look big in a focking circus tent.

The next thing, roysh, my eyes suddenly sting. I ask how long does it take for mace to clear and Sorcha says she doesn't know, but she's sure it's karma for what I did to my mum.

'Okay, *ssshhh*!' Erika suddenly goes and she's shushing me because Trevion has suddenly arrived and he's not supposed to *know* anything about the dress before the big day?

We're in Il Cielo, in case you care, on Burton Way.

He leans down and the old dear kisses him.

He's there, 'So, did you get a dress?'

Sorcha's like, 'Yes, she did. And don't ask any questions about it, Trevion. It's bad luck to know.'

I'm not sure if that's true. I knew fock-all about her dress before *our* wedding and we were in trouble before the bisque arrived.

I'm there, 'Er, is nobody else going to point out the obvious here? You can't *get* married, not while you're still married to the old man. So what's the point in even buying a dress? It could be, like, years before you're divorced. And God knows what size you'll be by then.'

Sorcha's there, 'Ross!'

Trevion looks at me like he wants to pull my legs off and beat me to death with them, and he probably would if there weren't witnesses. *She* still orders the *scialatielli*, I notice.

Then she goes, 'There's nothing to say we can't have a non-legal ceremony to demonstrate our commitment to one another.'

And she's serious.

I'm there, 'When? Where? What are you talking about?'

'Vegas,' *he* goes.

'Vegas? As in *Las* Vegas?'

'That's right, Ginger. You got a problem with that?'

'When are we talking?'

'Next weekend.'

I end up just laughing. It's, like, I *have* to? 'Let me guess,' I go. 'It just so happens to be the exact same day as Christian's casino is opening?'

No one answers.

I laugh again. 'This is all Johnny Sarno's idea, isn't it? Ross is going to Vegas anyway. Why not set up, like, a sham wedding for his old dear while he's there – see how he reacts. Can I just say, I wonder what the old man's going to think of it?'

She goes, 'Well, why don't you ask him? He's coming.'

I'm there, 'You invited him?'

Erika looks suddenly worried.

The old dear goes, 'Don't worry, Darling, he's coming on his own.'

Erika just nods, but at the same time she looks kind of sad?

Sorcha's phone suddenly rings. It must be serious, roysh, because she gets up and walks away from the table to take it.

'So what do MTV want?' I go, looking at Trevion. 'Me standing at the back of the church objecting?'

The old dear's like, 'I don't remember telling you that you were invited, Ross.'

I'm there, 'Oh, I'll be there – one way or the other. It'll be worth it just to watch you hobbling up the aisle on your focked ankle.'

Sorcha arrives back. She's got a look of, like, total shock on her face. 'That was . . . Bob Soto,' she goes. She looks like she's not going to be able to get the words out. 'Cillian . . .'

I watch Erika make a grab for her hand.

'Cillian's . . . been sacked,' she finally goes, which comes as no great surprise, although the rest of them crack on that it *does*?

'Bob has been – oh my God – *so* understanding – giving him time off so Cillian could get his head straight. But he said last night's show was, like, the last straw? That stuff about the major banks and corporations looking for money from the public purse – he said it was Communist talk. He said he could tolerate most things in life – but not Communism . . .'

'Some of us fought wars against those bastids,' Trevion goes, suddenly angry. 'I died a hundred fucking times fighting them.'

The old dear puts, like, a consoling orm around him.

Sorcha goes, 'Bob said they've revoked his work visa,' and I'm like, 'So what are you going to do?' and she's there, 'I don't know,' except that, deep down, I think she actually *does*?

What ends up happening is this. We forget about the meal. The old dear and Trevion offer to collect Honor from the crèche and the three of us – we're talking me, Sorcha and Erika – drive back to the gaff.

There's, like, total silence in the cor? It's like we all know what's coming. I'm tempted to point out that I was the one who said it wouldn't work, but for once in my life I keep the old Von Trapp shut.

He's home as well. The Prius is in the driveway. I automatically laugh. I never thought about it before, roysh, but its emissions are no better than the latest generation of small diesel cor, which cost half the price and are probably cooler to be seen in.

In a weird way, I think, I'm actually looking forward to this?

Johnny Sarno's already there ahead of us. God, he's good.

'Are you sure you want us there with you?' Erika goes, and Sorcha's like, 'I really don't want to be left on my own with him,' and with the shit he's been coming out with lately, you couldn't really *blame* her?

He's in their bedroom, believe it or not, packing.

'Sorcha,' he goes, 'I've been trying to get you on the phone.'

She's there, 'I already know, Cillian. Bob Soto rang.'

He cops me and Erika standing either side of her, roysh, and it's like he immediately knows?

You can see him still not wanting to believe it, though.

'We've got to go home,' he goes. 'But it's not the end of the world. I can put the message out just as effectively from home. I was thinking of setting up my own blog . . .'

I actually laugh out loud. A blog? It's almost, like, *too* funny?

He looks at the camera nervously.

'You need to start packing,' he goes. 'There's a flight at eight o'clock tonight.'

Sorcha's there, 'Cillian, I'm not going.'

This he again tries to ignore. He walks over to her, holds her by both shoulders and stares deep into her eyes. 'I'm especially worried about Ireland,' he goes. 'It's too reliant on a lot of shaky things continuing to support each other . . .'

She's there, 'Cillian, please . . .' and suddenly the tears stort to flow from, like, her eyes?

He's there, 'Our own economic growth has been sustained by high levels of consumption, which is dependent on high levels of borrowing, which is dependent on continuously increasing property values. But as soon as something happens to that market . . .'

'You're not listening!' Sorcha goes.

He suddenly stops.

She's there, 'Cillian, I don't know what's gotten into you. Or what you're mixed up in. But I don't want any part of it . . .'

'Don't tell me you're staying?'

'I'm happy here.'

'What,' he goes, 'appearing on some brain-dead TV programme that celebrates superficiality?'

I say fock-all. My attitude is, he's doing a good enough job hanging himself.

'I'm over here,' she goes in that real matter-of-fact way, '*trying* to come up with new ideas for my shop.'

He's there, 'Does it bother you that in two or three years time, you might not even have a shop? That Grafton Street could end up being a commercial wasteland?'

She shuts her eyes really tightly and shakes her head. The tears keep coming, though. 'I can't believe you'd say that to me,' she goes.

I take a step forward then. 'You'd, er, want to be hitting the road pretty soon,' I go, 'if you're going to make that flight. You're not in the Lamborghini anymore, remember?'

He's bulling, of course.

I hold out my hand and go, 'Keys?' meaning the keys to all the other rooms. Because the second he's gone, we're back living in a mansion again.

He tells me they're downstairs on the kitchen table.

He looks at Sorcha, obviously trying to come in from a different angle. 'What about Honor?' he goes. 'Will you say goodbye to her for me?'

I'm there, 'We'll do better than that. We'll say *adios*.'

He just nods. He's an auditor – he knows the bottom line. 'Well, goodbye,' he goes.

And then, suddenly, he's gone.

Sorcha literally collapses into Erika's orms, crying like I haven't seen her cry since . . . well, since *I* broke her hort. I'm so glad that Erika's here for her.

I wander over to the wardrobe to see has he left anything behind. There, sitting at the bottom, on their own, are his John Lobb custom brogues.

I sit on the side of the bed and try them on. They're, like, a perfect fit.

I'm driving home from tantric celibacy when, totally out of the blue, the poem 'Exposure' by Wilfred Owen pops into my head. I'm just thinking how it's structured in eight stanzas of equal length, each of which concludes with a short, emphatic statement or question that emphasizes the utter futility of war. The tone of the poem is depressing and negative. The language of the poem is bleak and Owen uses linguistic devices such as sibilance to help create an atmosphere of tension.

I haven't a clue what it means, of course – *or* what I'm supposed to do with it? But it's while I'm contemplating it that I decide to give Christian another try.

'Who?' the bird on the other end of the line goes. I'm talking about Martha, as in Christian's PA?

I'm there, 'Ross! O'Carroll! Kelly! The same Ross O'Carroll-Kelly who rang yesterday. And three times last week.'

'He didn't return your call?' she goes.

I'm there, 'No.'

She's like, 'He *has* been busy. Can I take your cell?'

I'm there, 'He *has* my, as you call it, cell. We've been mates since we were pretty much kids.'

'I'm sure, if he thought it was important, he would have called you. Just give me the cell again . . .'

And I do.

Like a fool, I do.

She's putting a brave boat on it. See, that's the Mountie way. *In te confido*, which literally means, 'Whatever!'

We're sitting in Mr Chow in Beverly Hills. Hilary Duff's never out of the place apparently. *And* Usher.

It's nice to get away from the cameras, just the three of us. Honor's eating her steamed dumplings, going, '*Eee, arr, sahn, ssuh, woo, liu, chi, bah, jeou, sher . . .*'

Still fock-all English. I'm thinking, at least when she goes back to Ireland, she'll be able to ask for directions in petrol stations.

Sorcha's BlackBerry beeps. Kate Bosworth was spotted arriving at the OmniPeace Charity Party in a dramatic Zac Posen with Yossi Harari bangles, although you can tell that Sorcha's hort's not really in it?

A waiter stops by, hears Honor babbling away and he goes, '*Ni hao ma?*' and Honor's like, '*Hen hao, xie xie,*' and the next thing, roysh, the two of them are having this pretty much conversation.

I'm just sitting there totally, I don't know, mesmerized if that's the word?

Sorcha barely even raises a smile. I feel like I should

suddenly say something, so I remind her that she's still a beautiful, intelligent girl – great face, amazing body – and without actually using the words 'fish in the sea', I tell her that one day she's going to meet someone who actually deserves her.

'You mean *you*?' she goes.

The funny thing is, I don't mean me at all. But I nod anyway. I'm happy to be her punchbag if it's a punchbag she needs right now. I owe her at least that.

I watch her give up on her crunchy snow pea sprouts, then for some reason my eyes sort of, like, stray over her left shoulder and I see a familiar face sitting three tables behind us.

At first, roysh, I'm thinking, no, it couldn't possibly be . . .

I keep watching her, just to be a hundred per cent sure.

'Sorcha,' I eventually go. 'Stella McCortney's sitting behind you.'

The colour immediately drains from her face. She's like, 'What?'

I'm there, 'Stella *actual* McCortney. She's having lunch just there – obviously tofu or some shit.'

Sorcha looks suddenly sad. 'Ross, this isn't like the time you rang me up pretending to be Maya Angelou saying thank you for the poem I sent her?'

'No, I swear.'

'Or the time you told me you saw Jane Goodall on TV giving cigarettes to a monkey?'

'Look, I apologized for that as well. I'm telling you, it's *the* Stella McCortney. Left hammer.'

She does that thing that birds do when they *think* they're being subtle? She pretends she's spotted a bit of, I don't know, lint on the shoulder of her See by Chloé T-shirt and as she's, like, sweeping it off with her hand, she has a quick look back.

She goes into what would have to be described as shock

337

then – as in, she turns back around to me with both hands up to her face and she's having palpitations. She's literally struggling to breathe. I'm telling her to calm down, that she's just another, I suppose, human being, though that's like saying that Brian O'Driscoll is just another rugby player or that Paris Hilton likes engagement presents.

'Drink some water,' I go, which she does. Then I reach across and put my hand on top of hers. I'm there, 'Be aware of your breathing,' passing on some of my yoga, I suppose you'd call it, wisdom?

'In . . . and out . . . in . . . and out . . .'

I get her calm again, roysh, then I go, 'We're going to go and focking talk to her.'

She shakes her head.

I'm there, 'Yes . . .'

'Ross, I wouldn't know what to say.'

She storts getting worked up again.

I'm there, 'You'll think of something.'

'I could tell her that she was *so* right about jumpsuits,' she goes. 'Halston, Marc Jacobs, Preen – they're all doing them this autumn. Or, no – I could tell her that I've got, like, *all* of her CARE range – even the Purifying Foaming Cleanser and the 5 Benefits Moisturizing Fluid?'

I'm there, 'Why don't you stort by saying hello? Then just be yourself, Sorcha. She'll focking love you – everyone does.'

I stand up. 'Look, I'm done with my food,' I go.

I pick Honor up, hold her in one orm, then I take Sorcha's hand and she stands up as well. I watch her take a deep breath. Then I go, 'Ready?' and she sort of, like, nods, then breathes out.

We tip over. Stella's on her Tobler. As we approach the table, I can feel Sorcha's hand tighten in mine.

It has to be said, roysh, that Stella is an absolute cracker. I always *thought* she was in photographs? But in real life, I have to tell you, she's even better.

Sorcha's there, 'Excuse me,' and Stella looks up.

'Oh, hello,' Stella goes, unbelievably friendly.

'My name's Sorcha and I'm from, like, Ireland? And I just want to say that you are my – oh my God – *total* inspiration.'

'What a lovely thing to say,' Stella goes.

Even though she hears it probably fifty times a day, she acts like it's the first time anyone's ever said it to her, which is a mork of, like, true class. She's even inspiring me and I've only just met the bird.

Then she's like, 'And what a beautiful baby,' and she stands up.

Sorcha goes, 'This is Honor. Honor, this is Stella McCortney.'

'*Ni hao ma*,' Honor goes.

Stella's, like, stroking Honor's cheek, going, 'How old is she?' and Sorcha's there, 'Nearly two,' and Stella goes, 'Oh, so she's putting sentences together?' and I'm there, 'None that you'd actually understand – she could probably talk you through the menu, though.'

She laughs, even though she probably doesn't really get the gag. 'And you're Sorcha's husband?' she goes, offering me her hand.

I'm about to go, 'Used to be,' but Sorcha gets in before me and goes, 'Yes, this is Ross,' which is nice, because she didn't *have* to say it?

Stella's there, 'Well, won't you sit down? I was about to have tea,' and of course Sorcha's face lights up like a skobie on the last Luas to Belgord.

'Sorcha,' I go, 'I'm going to take Honor out. She's getting a bit restless,' which is horseshit, of course. I just know that, given my form, I'd end up saying something to totally fock it up for her.

I make the shape of a phone with my hand and I go, 'Give me a ring and I'll come and get you,' and the look she gives, it'd almost make you want to be a nice goy all the time?

One of the things that's always been said about me is that I look really, really well with a tan. Which is why, at this moment in time, I'm out on the patio, catching a few rays before Vegas, where they're going to film, like, the series finale of *Ross, His Mother, His Wife and Her Lover.*

I'm reading an orticle about myself in *Weekly OK!* – some vegetarian shower are up in orms about the 'Real Women Eat Meat' T-shirt I was wearing in last week's episode and I'm praying that Stella didn't see it – otherwise the internship that she's promised Sorcha could be out the focking window.

I can hear voices coming from the kitchen – Erika and my old dear having the DMCs. The old dear's going, 'I know what Ross thinks. He thinks I'm doing it for the benefit of the cameras. For the publicity. But it's not, Erika. I'm so in love. I know he's old and I don't know how many years he has left. But somehow that makes our time together all the more precious.'

I actually feel like puking again.

She gives a little girly giggle. 'He's so self-conscious about his face . . . I've told him a hundred times that it doesn't matter to me. And it really doesn't. I've always been more interested in what lies beneath. My first boyfriend, Conor, he was a frightful-looking thing. Still is – I saw him on television not so long ago, at Leopardstown. And as for your father . . .'

She lets it just hang there.

Erika's there, 'I suppose that's *one* thing I should be grateful to her for – unlike Ross, I got my mum's looks, not his.'

They both laugh, then eventually the old dear goes, 'It was *my* fault, you know.'

Erika's like, 'What?'

'You being brought up thinking someone else was your father . . .'

'It was *her* fault, Fionnuala. She was my mother.'

'She would have done the right thing – and your father would have done the right thing – had I not given him that ultimatum. I was convinced I was losing my mind. I *did* lose it . . .'

'It's still not your fault,' Erika goes.

The old dear's there, 'I'm going to tell you a story. And this'll be my last word on the subject. But I had no relationship with my mother. She went insane when I was, well . . . not long after I was born . . .'

'I'm sorry . . .'

'It's okay. My father used to take me to see her every Sunday in what we used to call Mummy's House. It was a – oh, God forgive me – a bloody nuthouse. And we'd sit there for a couple of hours talking to this woman and I'd wonder why she never talked back. Why she never even seemed to see us . . .'

I realize that she's crying.

'I still go, from time to time,' she goes.

Erika's there, 'She's still alive?'

'Well – *if* that's what you consider alive. I go there and I sit opposite her and most of the time I don't even say anything. We just sit looking at each other. I don't know what I'm waiting for. Just some flicker of recognition, I suppose. Crazy, I know. But I would give up everything I have, Erika – everything! – just for one conversation with her. Just to say, 'Hello, Mum,' and have her say, 'Hello, Fionnuala,' and then to tell her that, in spite of everything, it all worked out in the end, because look at me – I'm happy . . .'

I can hear Erika crying, too.

'If you live to be my age,' the old dear goes, 'I can assure you, Darling, you're going to have lots and lots of regrets. Just make sure, if it's at all possible, that they're regrets you can live with . . .'

That's the thing about my old dear. If you let her, she could actually have you feeling sorry for her?

'The good news,' I go, 'is that *he's* gone,' meaning Cillian.

Ro knows who I'm talking about – he's a smort kid.

'Don't un I know,' he goes. 'He's home – he's after being in all the papers, saying all sorts. The wurdled's gonna end, according to him. They're calling him Dr Doom.'

I laugh. They're unbelievably quick the way they come up with these names.

'Well,' I go, 'she's a lot happier without him, I can tell you that. The other major news is that your, I suppose, grand-mother is getting married – you'll be here for that.'

'Maddied?' he goes. 'Is she not still maddied to me grannda?'

I'm there, 'She is. It's actually just a sham wedding? They're only doing it for the cameras. Anyway, did your old dear book your ticket?'

'She did, yeah.'

'So what day are you arriving?'

'Er, Toorsday – seven in the night.'

'Cool – what's the flight number.'

'It's, er, EI EIO.'

I write it down.

He's there, 'Anyway, Rosser, I'd better go,' and he quickly hangs up.

At that exact point, roysh, a bird walks past – she's kind of, like, a cross between Kristin Cavallari and Adrienne Bailon – and she checks my boat out in a serious way.

'I'm Ross,' I automatically go. 'You clearly like what you see.'

She just laughs and goes, 'Your nose is bleeding.'

I'm like, 'It's what?' and I put my finger up to it and it ends up being red. I'm there, 'What the fock?'

She goes, '*Eeewww!*' and turns her head away and I'm there thinking, I wonder is that supposed to happen?

So I finally find him, sitting outside Newsroom, where we had our first – okay, if you want to call it that – *date*, drinking another one of his famous Taiwanese milk teas. I have nothing rehearsed, but I've always been good in, like, situations, especially when it comes to talking my way out of them.

I sit down opposite him and I go, 'Okay, I focked up in a major way. And I just want to say, you know, sorry, blahdy blahdy blah. I'd have to say, in my defence, I'm not used to having gay friends. I was probably just a bit, I don't know, homophobic, if you want to call it that. So, basically, sorry – and it's not often I say that . . .'

He sort of, like, screws up his face and goes, 'Ross? Ross, is that you?'

Which throws me a bit. I'm there, 'Er, yeah.'

'Oh my God,' he goes, 'your *nose!*' and he grabs me by the shoulder and sort of, like, turns me to the side, to see it from *another* angle? 'It's . . .'

I laugh. I totally forgot that he hasn't, like, seen it yet. I'm there, 'Go on, what?'

'It's . . . *stunning*,' he goes.

I think that's one of the things I've really missed about Harve – the way he's always bigging me up?

'You want to check out the bod?' I go. He smiles. I grab his hand and place it on my left pec, then guide it slowly across my chest and down my washboard stomach. 'Oh! My! God!'

he goes. I think he really appreciates that there's no way I'd do that if I was really ashamed to have him as, like, a mate. 'You are *so* ripped!'

I'm there, 'Thanks.'

'Your eyes are still quite bloodshot,' he goes.

I'm there, 'Yeah, no, don't worry about that – that's where Erika sprayed me with mace.'

'She sprayed you with mace?'

'Yeah, she thought I was going to hop her. Hop them all – Sorcha and my old dear included.'

He looks at me, sort of, like, worried?

'So am I forgiven?' I go and he just smiles, being obviously a sucker for a pretty face, and I order a Taiwanese milk tea, just to show him it's still the same old me.

I'm like, 'The point I was trying to make just there – to break it down for you and blahdy blah – was that I do want you as a friend. And fock what the press think.'

He's obviously delighted. 'I *was* going to call you,' he goes, acting all bashful. 'I've been doing a lot of thinking as well . . .'

I never said I'd been doing a *lot* of thinking, but I let it go.

For some reason, roysh, I look down and I notice the bags at his feet. He's there, 'I mean, who am I to lecture you about your attitudes when I haven't properly faced up to who *I* am?'

I'm suddenly speechless.

'I'm going to go see my parents,' he goes.

I'm like, 'Whoa! Are you absolutely sure about this?' suddenly feeling guilty for having, like, pushed him. 'I mean, are you not scared?'

'Yeah, I'm scared,' he goes. 'But since when has that been an excuse for not doing something?'

I shake my head. See, he thinks he's learned a lot from me – it's actually the other way around?

344

'If they love me,' he goes, 'they'll accept it. Either way, I can't go on living a lie.'

I'm there, 'You tinkering with cors? Doing the voice?'

'Exactly. It's, like, *so* exhausting.'

He asks me how Sorcha is and I tell him not bad, considering everything. 'You know she gave *him* the road?'

He's like, 'Cillian? I saw last week's show. That letter to George Bush was, like, so funny.'

I'm there, 'Yeah – but only up to a point. I'm glad he's gone, though. There's no way someone like him was going to keep her happy, especially with me there putting pressure on him.'

'Is she upset?'

'Let's just say she's getting over it. Stella McCortney's offered her a job.'

He laughs like he can't actually believe it. 'Stella?' he keeps going. '*The* Stella?'

'Yeah, we met her in a restaurant and they just hit it off. Well, you know Sorcha. People just fall in love with her. Then she had, like, a formal interview. So you can imagine, we were up at, like, five in the morning. All the drama. Should should wear her Issa "Lucky" day dress with a Ritmo watch or her Express tunic dress with Kara Ross cuffs and her Anya Hindmarch clutch . . .'

'Which did she choose in the end?' he goes, sitting forward, genuinely interested.

I'm like, 'Neither. She actually wore a navy cap-sleeve dress by Burberry with her petrol-blue Robert Sanderson pump heels . . .'

'That is *such* a good look for her! Will you tell her I said that was *such* a good look for her?'

I'm like, of course – it's the least I can do.

I tell him I'm driving to Vegas this afternoon. I can't wait to see Ro. He asks me if I'm coming back to LA again. I tell him I don't really know my plans yet, but deep down I think we both realize that this is goodbye.

I'm actually a lot sadder than I thought I'd be, although I try to put, like, a brave face on it? 'The thing is,' I go, 'I'm not sure if it's ever *really* goodbye these days, when it's all Facebook, texting, blahdy blahdy blah.'

He smiles. He knows this is my whole macho act, just as *I* know how absolutely hopeless I am at keeping in touch.

I feel, like, a sudden heaviness in my chest and I'm suddenly taking a huge interest in an oil stain on the tablecloth, going, 'That's not going to come out easily.'

Then I look up and notice that Harvey is bawling his eyes out and I realize that's it's alright for me to cry, too.

We end up just throwing our orms around each other, then after hugging for maybe twenty – at the very most thirty seconds – he pulls back, looks me straight in the eye and tells me that he loves me. And I think, fock it, and I tell him – you know what? – I love him, too.

And then I leave him where I first found him – on Robertson Boulevard, looking great.

Father Fehily used to tell us that some friendships are for a particular time. He used to say, is a butterfly any less beautiful if it lives for only one day?

I stort the cor and pretty soon he's just a speck in my rearview. Then I'm back on the road, the tears flowing freely now and me wiping them away with, like, the palm of my hand.

It's maybe the tenth time I've heard the story, but, to be honest, she could tell me a hundred times more if she wants. It's a long time since I've seen her this happy.

'I told her all about my shop back home and she asked me about my plans for it. I was like, "Oh my God, I've thought of *so* many over here, I can't *actually* decide? But I definitely want to do Tracy Reese, Anna Sui, Pedro Garcia, Kooba, Tibi, Chaiken, Gryphon and CC Skye. Oh, and Rich & Skinny. I can't believe that no one in Ireland is *doing* Rich & Skinny."

'And she was like, "But what do you really want to do?" and I was thinking, like I always do, WWSD? Is she talking about Charlotte Ronson? Or Rag & Bone? Or something totally outside of the box, like Tolani scarves, because no one's doing those either? Then she goes, "In your heart, Sorcha," and – oh my God – it was like she *knew*, Ross. It was like she could see into my soul.'

I'm there, 'Cool.'

It's, like, one o'clock and I'm going to have to be heading off soon if I'm going to meet Ronan off that flight. We're sitting on the edge of the pool, with our legs dangling in the water. I'm holding Honor and she's chatting away in her usual gibberish. Erika's inside, on the phone, finally talking to her old dear – they've been on for, like, three hours, which has to be good. *My* old dear and Trevion are having lunch in Il Sole with Johnny and a few of the other MTV heads, planning this shambles of a wedding.

'So tell me again,' I go, 'what happened next?' even though I *know*.

'I just started telling her about my dream – which I'd told absolutely no one about before – to start up my own clothing line that allows you to *dress* thin and yet *be* healthy? Blazers that skim the hips, jeans with low back pockets to lift your bum and thicker heels that de-emphasize the ankles.

'Oh my God, I was on fire, Ross. I started coming out with all this stuff. Jewelled necklines take centre-stage away from less-than-toned mid-sections. Open peep-toe sandals elongate and slim the lower half of the body. Even something as simple as a portrait collar and belt can transform uneven proportions into an hourglass figure . . .'

She suddenly stops, looking, I don't know, embarrassed by her excitement. Or maybe she's waiting for me to burst her bubble.

I tell her I think it's a great idea.

She's there, 'Really?'

I'm like, 'Yeah.'

'It's just that, for girls, weight is *so* connected to self-esteem. But there are ways of dressing ten pounds lighter without *actually* starving yourself?'

Deep down, I know she's thinking about Aoife. I doubt she ever stops thinking about her.

We're both quiet then and it's nice. 'Can I say something to you?' she eventually goes.

I'm there, 'Yeah.'

'When you and I broke up, I really thought it was the end of everything. I never thought I'd end up with *the* most amazing friend in the world.'

And it's incredible, roysh, because I tell her I *thought* the reason I originally came to LA was to try to, like, win her back. Now I know it wasn't. I came here just to try to make things right. She reaches for my hand and she tells me that I have.

Then she goes, 'Why don't you give Honor some of that?'

See, I'm eating, like, a Payday? 'But it's actual chocolate,' I go.

She smiles. 'I'm sure it won't do her any harm.'

I break her off a piece and I'm there, 'Look, Honor – chocolate,' and she goes at it like a focking sailor on shore-leave.

The next I hear is the sound of someone making their way down from the gaff. I sort of, like, *half* turn around?

It's Erika. 'Hey,' she goes.

She kicks off her flip-flops and sits down beside us, her feet in the pool.

We're both like, 'Hey,' then Sorcha asks her if everything's okay.

Erika just nods.

I look at her, roysh, and it's amazing because for the very first time I can honestly say that she does nothing for me. No yoga, no tricks. I just don't fancy her, even though she *does* have incredible legs.

'They're both coming over,' she goes. 'I'm going to meet them in Vegas – Charles *and* Mum.'

In other words, Helen and Dick Features. She's smiling – she seems to be happy. I tell her that's great, although I don't let her know my true feelings, of course.

She asks me when I'm leaving and I tell her now. She says she can't wait to see Ro and she's not the only one. It's, like, there's already a buzz, just around the fact that he's coming.

I stand up and tell them I'd better get going. I hand Honor to Sorcha, then I give them each – I suppose you could call them the three women in my life – a hug and a peck on each cheek and I tell them I'll see them in a couple of days.

I'm, like, ten feet away from the house when I hear Honor go, 'Chocolate, Daddy! Chocolate!'

I turn back and smile. It might be the happiest I've ever been.

Ronan's not on flight EI EIO. In fact, there *is* no flight EI EIO.

I'm standing in the arrivals hall of McCarron airport and I'm scanning the board, thinking maybe he just got the number orseways, still prepared to give him the benefit of the doubt, the little focker. But there's nothing coming in from New York at 7.00 p.m. and I suddenly know how all those birds I've scored on holidays must feel when they find out there's no 1 Main Street, Dublin.

I whip out my phone and ring his number. He answers – he has the *actual* balls to answer – and all I can hear in the background is, like, *beep beep beep* and then *ding aling aling* and of course there's no even *need* to ask him where he is? Except I do ask, because I'm his father.

'I'm in a little carpet joint Downtown,' he goes, as casual as that. 'Here, there's a fella here, Rosser – I'm after been watching him. He's betting lavender chips – five hundred large – and he always guesses right. Do you think he's part of the skim?'

I'm there, 'I don't know. I don't even know what you're talking about. What *I* want to know is, why aren't you at the airport?'

'Ah, I got in a bit early,' he goes.

I'm there, 'How early?'

'Depends – would you count today as a full day?'

'Ronan!'

'Alright, keep your knickers on. Three days.'

'Three *days*?'

'But that *is* counting today as a full day.'

'You've been in Vegas for three days? A ten-year-old boy? On his own?'

'Ah,' he goes, 'you're never on yisser own in this town. No, what happened was, I wanted to get the lie of the land before you got here,' and then I hear him suddenly shout – I don't know at who – 'Hey, what kind of bull feathers is this? I said two-fifty large!'

I'm there, 'Are you gambling? Tell me you're not gambling.'

'Don't sweat it, Rosser,' he goes, 'Luck's running against the house tonight.'

I'm there, 'Running against the house?' and I'm thinking, this is Tina, letting him watch whatever the fock he wants on TV and hang around with criminal types three times his age.

'Ro,' I go, 'get the fock out of there now. And I mean it,' and he's suddenly quiet. He knows when I'm being serious, in fairness to him. I'm there, 'Go to the hotel and wait for me there.'

'I'll tell you what,' he goes, 'I'm just going to stick me head into Caesars on the way back up. Meet me there. I'll be mooching around,' and then he just hangs up on me.

I'm straight back to the cor lot and you can imagine how actually pissed off I am. The traffic on the Strip is murder and it takes me, like, an hour to get there and, of course, the whole way I'm thinking, if they find a kid on the gaming floor, they'll call the cops.

I swing up outside, practically throw the keys at the valet and peg it in.

Caesars is humungous. There must be, like, five thousand people in there, milling around, literally all human life, we're talking rich-looking dudes in ten-grand suits, we're talking fat mums and dads with their fat kids, we're talking stunning-looking birds wearing half-nothing, a fair few of them giving me the elevator eyes, although I don't give them anything back, which shows you how worried I am.

The place smells of tequila, *Issey Miyake* and sweat and I'm being deafened by the sound of polyphonic music and bells and whistles and, every ten seconds or so, someone some-where cheers and I run to where the noise is coming from, thinking – from past experience – that he's bound to be at the centre of it, but this time he never is.

I'm trying his number, but it's going straight to message-minder, which means it's off.

I head for the area where the machines are, remembering

how much he used to love those ones with the moving floors that you stuck a coin in and tried to send, like, an avalanche of money into the chute. He was forever kicking those. I couldn't tell you how many times I've had the call from the lads in Quirkey's telling me to come and pick him up.

He's not there. It's mostly elderly women, sitting on high stools, feeding coins into machines and hitting buttons without even looking at the screen.

Then I remember him on the phone, banging about the ball and wheel, so I head for the roulette tables.

I see a man in a stetson dropping chips all over the grid – he must have every focking number on the wheel covered. The last time I saw a man in a stetson was in Lidl in Arklow. His wife checks me out in a major way and sips her margarita, imagining – I can always tell – that the straw is actually me.

I push on. Again, no interest.

I head for the craps tables. Ro's always had, like, a thing for dice and he carries around a lucky one that Martin 'The Viper' Foley's supposed to have had in his pocket when he survived the third attempt on his life – or maybe even fourth.

There's, like, no sign of him there either, just mostly gangs of goys – a lot of stag porties, I'd imagine – shouting and generally giving it loads.

I'm actually on the point of giving up when I finally cop him. He's leaning against a pillar, staring at these four dudes playing blackjack, roysh, and at the same time he's, like, chatting to himself, except it's like he's making, I don't know, calculations in his head.

I morch straight over to him, roysh, grab him by the shoulder and sort of, like, spin him around, obviously catching him by surprise. 'What the fock do you think you're doing?' I go.

He looks at me like I'm the TV licence inspector he's been brought up to fear.

He's there, 'Who the fook are you?' and I realize all of a sudden that he genuinely *doesn't* know?

But I don't get a chance to explain about my nose. Because the next thing I know, something hits me square in the chest, the wind is taken out of me and I'm all of a sudden on the deck, flat on my face, with what feels like the entire Munster pack on top of me.

It's like the entire casino is suddenly quiet and I don't know whether it's because everyone's watching or because I'm dead.

Then I think I can't be dead – because of the pain. My orms are pinned behind my back and someone's applying pressure to them and it feels like they're going to, like, snap off. And I can't even beg for mercy, roysh, because I haven't a focking breath.

I'm lying there, if I'm being honest, waiting to feel the bones just break.

'Hang on a second,' I hear Ronan suddenly go. 'Ah, sure, it's Rosser – here, let him up, Man,' and the next thing I know, my orms are suddenly released and I'm lifted – *literally* lifted – back to my feet.

I turn around, roysh, still dizzy, and there, standing next to Ro, is this humungous focker, who's as wide as he is tall – and he must be six-foot-eight – his body so ripped that his suit looks like a focking lagging jacket. He's like something out of *The Sopranos*. He's got dork, greased-back hair and a face as ugly as Darndale and twice as dangerous.

He's late forties, early fifties maybe, but he could give Martin Johnson a wedgie and make the focker say thanks.

Ronan's laughing. He's there, 'What happened to your nose, Rosser?'

I touch it, just to double-check it's still there. I'm there, 'Never mind that – who's this guy?'

The rest of the casino goes back to its own business again.

'This is Big Juice,' Ronan goes.

I'm there, 'Big Juice? Er, I think I'm going to need *more* than that?'

Big Juice sticks out his hand. 'Anthony Trombino,' he goes.

My hand just, like, disappears into his.

'He's a minder,' Ronan goes. 'You can rent them. Three hundred snots a day. Nudger and Gull got him for me as a surprise.'

I'm wondering will he ever have friends with *actual* names?

'I *should* be pissed off,' I go, then I look at Big Juice. 'But at least someone's been looking after him. Thanks.'

He's there, 'Hey, forget about it,' except he says it like it's one long word, the way they say it on TV.

Ronan goes, 'Here, watch this, Rosser,' and he points at me and goes, 'Hey, Big Juice, this fella here's wising off at me, so he is.'

Big Juice looks at me, roysh, straight in the eye and goes, 'I'm going to ask you nicely, Sir – step away or I will feed you your *fucking* teeth . . .'

My body literally shivers.

Ronan laughs. 'He's the fooken business, isn't he, Rosser?'

I'm there, 'Er, yeah, he's the business.'

'He's grandda was Joey Trombino – had points in every casino with a fooken horse book. And he's da was Jake Trombino. He was a fooken button man for Lefty Rosenthal . . .'

I'm there, 'I have to say, I'm pretty sure I'd have ridden the tackle had I seen it coming,' and Big Juice just nods. He says he's sure I would, which *is* nice of him.

'He knew them all,' Ronan goes. 'Benny Siegel, Meyer Lansky, Frank Costello, all them boys . . . What was the other fella?'

'Lucky Luciano,' Big Juice goes.

'Lucky Luciano! Ah, he's some fooken stories as well. Here, tell Rosser about Mad Sam Spilotro . . .'

'It's late,' I go, cutting him off. 'It's late – and it's been, well, a long day for me . . .'

'Point taken,' Ronan goes. 'You go get yourself some shut-eye, Rosser. Me and Big Juice are going to take the party on to Private Eyes, a little club I know.'

I'm there, 'Private Eyes, my hole – you're coming with me,' and he sort of, like, rolls his eyes at Big Juice and says it was woorth a try, in anyhow.

'I'll see you tomorrow,' Big Juice goes, then he turns to me and says, provided that's okay. 'I been paid up to the end of the week,' he goes.

I look at Ronan's little face and of course I *can't* say no? I'm there, 'Er, cool, yeah.'

'Moostard,' Ronan goes.

As we're walking away, roysh, Big Juice grabs my orm – he can put his entire hand around my bicep and still his fingers touch – and he tells me that that's one smart kid I got. I tell him I know – that's what frightens me.

Ten minutes later, we're in the cor – just me and Ro – out on the Strip, heading for the *Star Wars* Casino, where Ronan tells me he's already checked in.

'Big Juice!' I can't help but go, shaking my head.

We've got the top down. It's, like, a muggy night.

'He's the business, isn't he, Rosser?' Ronan goes.

I'm there, 'Yes, he's the business.'

'You'd know not to fook with him, wouldn't you? See, in my line of work, it pays to advertise.'

I'm there, 'Only you,' and I laugh – I suppose at, like, the good of it?

He laughs as well. 'He fooken floored you but, didn't you, Rosser?'

'Yeah,' I end up having to go.

'Like a sack of fooken spuds.'

He's suddenly serious. 'You're not going to tell me ma, are you?'

'So she thinks you've been here with me the whole time?'

'Er, yeah.'

I think Tina's the only person in the world he's *actually* scared of?

'I'll tell you what,' I go. 'I won't tell her *if* you promise not to pull a stunt like that again. I worry about you, Ro.'

'Ah, I'm wide, Rosser.'

'I know you're wide. And I know you're, like, way more intelligent than me, even though you're only, like, ten. It doesn't mean I don't still worry about you.'

'Okay.'

'Honestly, I don't care what you get up to – just don't leave me in the dork. There's been too many secrets in our family.'

'Okay.'

The next thing, roysh, we're stopped at a red light at the junction of The Strip and Flamingo Road. I'm looking at the fountains of the Bellagio, the ones you see on, like, *Ocean's Eleven*?

There's, like, a gang of heads on the corner and they're mostly – and I don't know if this is racist – but black. Two or three of them stort walking over towards the car and – again, this is racist – I'm suddenly kacking it.

I'm thinking, will I just nail the accelerator here?

It's only when they come closer that I realize they're basically handing out concessions for, like, clubs and then, like, escort services as well? They've got this way of, like, holding the cords between two fingers and flicking them with a thumbnail, so they make, like, a *ffftt, ffftt* sound and they're also going, 'Girls! Girls! You want girls?'

One of them goes to hand me a cord, roysh, and I'm just about to go, 'Sorry – black or not – I'm actually here with my son?' when he suddenly turns around and goes, 'Hey, Ronan – *what's de stareee?*' and offers him the high-five.

Ronan goes, 'Alright, boys?' and then he sort of, like, flicks his head at me, presumably to say, 'Get out of here – I'm with the oul' fella.'

The light turns green and I step on the accelerator. There's a squeal from my tyres and the three – again – black dudes jump back in fright.

Of course, I'm left shaking my head again, but this time not in a good way?

'Ah, they just know me from walking up and down The Strip,' Ronan goes, as I'm pulling into the casino cor pork.

I'm there, 'Ro, forget what I said about secrets. There's shit I don't actually *want* to know?'

10. Vegas, Baby

I tend to do a lot of my – I suppose you'd have to call it – deep thinking while I'm shaving. So there I am, roysh, staring into the mirror, and it's suddenly going through my head how much I've missed the goys and how much I'm looking forward to hanging out with them again. They flew in last night and I'm trying to work out how long it's been since I last saw them. We're talking November to the end of June – you do the maths.

Ronan's outside the door, telling me that the Nevada Gaming Commission are on his case – or, more specifically, busting his balls, over what he calls his 'associations'.

'Oh, no,' I go, 'not again,' because sometimes you've got to just, like, play along? It can be good sometimes for kids to have an imagination.

'Piece-of-shit motherfuckers,' he goes, 'saw me having breakfast with Solly Abrams and Santo Trafficante! At the Dunes! Ah, you know how that goes.'

'So that's, like, a bad thing, is it?' I shout out to him.

'What have you got, rocks in your head? Everyone knows they're wiseguys.'

'Of course – I forgot.'

I finish up and wipe the rest of the foam off my face.

'I wouldn't mind,' Ronan goes, 'but I'm the one trying to keep the fucken peace out here. Phil Profaci's gone kill-crazy. You know Blowtorch Phil?'

'I know the face,' I go. 'I've never heard the name.'

'Well, he's *supposed* to be the outfit's outside man here –

shouldn't be *on* the floor. Anyway, two nights ago, he has a bad night at the craps table. You know Abie Zwillman? Best fucken stickman *on* The Strip. Abie's been with me for thirty years. Phil breaks his fucken arm, then tells Johnny Guzak, the pit boss, to tear up his marker or he'll melt his fucken face – I'm talking about a marker for twenty large here . . .'

I slap on the old Kiehls.

'Then, he hits the bar,' Ronan goes, 'gets all liquored up, comes back, busts his way into the soft count room and walks out with a caseful of big ones . . .'

And the old *Gaultier* the Sequel.

'So anyway, they've decided to take him out. Giuseppe Bonnaro and Tony the Ant are flying in. He gets a shave every morning in the barber shop at the Silver Slipper. Phil's sweet on one of the broads there – ah, she's up in the paints age-wise, but she still knows a few tricks . . .'

I step out of the bathroom. I'm there, 'Can I just ask, Ro – we *are* just bantering here, aren't we?' because it *does* always pay to check with him.

'Course we are,' he goes. 'Ah, it's just I been listening to Big Juice and he's stories. I'm telling you, the fellas over here, Rosser, back in the day, thee'd put the boys back home in the fooken ha'penny place.'

I'm actually pulling on my green Apple Crumble, roysh, which is maybe why I stort to feel suddenly patriotic? And it's weird, roysh, because I'm the one suddenly *defending* Ireland? 'What about The Genoddle?' I go. 'The Penguin? The Monk?'

It's actually the mention of The Monk that gets him. He stares into the distance and smiles. It's nice to see he's still a major fan.

'Here,' he goes then, 'I need to talk to you about this wrinkle I'm after coming up with.'

I don't know what a wrinkle is, but it doesn't sound *very*

legal? I check my phone. I've got, like, a text from JP. They're actually out on The Strip. He's like, 'Hav u seen this thng?' presumably meaning the *Star Wars* Casino and I suddenly realize that I haven't. We came in the back way last night and, because Ro already had the key, we went straight up to the room in the lift – or elevator, if you want to call it that.

I turn around to Ro and I'm like, 'The goys are outside – why don't you tell me while we're walking?' which is exactly what he ends up doing.

'See, I'm after been examining traditional algorithms and equations which describe various kinds of wheels and spindles,' he's going. 'For example,

$$V^2 = \frac{Wrad^2}{k\,(4C + md^2)}$$

which is a cracking little equation for figuring out the speed of the wheels of a train . . .'

We pick Big Juice up in the lobby. It's, like, mayhem down there – loads of *Star Wars* characters milling around. I spot three or four Jar Jar Binkses serving drinks, although I'm pretty sure they're called Gungans.

Ronan's still going. 'Using a Markov chain – a stachostic model describing a sequence of possible events in which the probability of each event depends only on the state attained in the previous event – it's possible to predict, with great accuracy, what a ball will eventually do, based on the first few seconds of the spin . . .'

I hear Big Juice tell him that it's the best scam he's heard since Tony 'Big Tuna' Collovati took the Hacienda for seven-hundred-and-fifty large and I'm thinking, I'll definitely have to ring Nudger and Gull to tell them that, whatever they paid, they really got their money's worth with this dude.

They're waiting in front of the place – we're talking Oisinn,

It's like I've suddenly been punched in the chest. I try to say something, but I can't actually speak. Christian puts the little goy in my orms and I sit there just staring at him while he looks up at me. He even smiles.

'Hey,' Christian goes, 'he likes you.'

I have that feeling you get sometimes, that if I open my mouth to speak, I'm just going to, like, break down?

I have to just hand the little goy back to Lauren, jump up off the sofa and literally run for the door. 'Where are you going?' Christian goes, but I don't even answer.

The next thing I know, roysh, I'm pegging it past Sand-people and Bounty Hunters, past tables full of Jedis and Sith playing Texas Hold 'Em and a Biker Scout giving out shit to a croupier and I'm thinking how I have to find him before he makes this terrible, terrible mistake. A bird in a Princess Leia slave-girl outfit asks me if I want my champagne topped up, but I don't even answer. I keep running towards the West Tower and the elevator that will take me to *his* room, hoping against hope that I'm not too late.

I *am* too late. The door's open and I can hear voices inside the room, even from down the corridor. Sorcha and the old man – one saying that the chap must be suffering from post-traumatic stress disorder, capitals P through D, the other saying that the whole thing is like, *Oh my God!*

'What's going on?' I go, standing in the doorway, cracking on not to know.

They all look at me at exactly the same time. The old man is pacing the floor. Sorcha and Helen are sitting on the edge of the bed, either side of the old dear, who's already in her wedding dress – even though the ceremony's, like, hours away – and she's got, like, tears streaming out of her eyes, making shit of her make-up.

Erika's there as well. It's actually Erika who goes, 'Trevion's gone, Ross.'

Her and Sorcha's dresses are nice actually. They must have all been having a final dress rehearsal when they found out.

I'm there, 'Gone? What do you mean, gone?'

The old man's there, 'Decided he couldn't go through with it and had it away, like the proverbial thief in the night.'

He really does love the sound of his own voice.

'I'm sorry,' I go, actually being sincere. 'As in, sorry to hear?'

The old dear just looks up at me – an Emo gone wrong – but she doesn't *say* shit? She just, like, stares me out of it.

The old man's there, 'You didn't say something to him, did you, Ross?'

I'm like, 'Meaning?'

'Well, it's just I saw the pair of you having a *tête-à-tête*, pardon the French, last night. Well, I was just telling your mother. It was immediately after – Trevion walked over to bar, *knocked back* his bourbon – as they say in the movies – and said that's it, he was gone. I said, "Well, this is a fine how-do-you-do – you bowing out of your stag at, what, half-eleven?" He gave me a good old hug and he said, "Goodbye, Charlie." At the time, I thought he meant goodnight – the whiskey talking and so forth. But no. Came to check on him about an hour ago and he was gone . . .'

'Fock!'

'Leaving nothing but a note.'

'A note?' I look at the old dear and I'm like, 'Er, what did it actually say?' trying *not* to sound worried? 'As in, were there any clues in it, as to why he, you know, whatever . . .'

Sorcha answers for her. 'Ross, I think that's between your mum and Trevion, don't you?'

The old dear hasn't taken her eyes off me for the last thirty seconds and the way she's looking at me, roysh, it's as if she's trying to read my face? And what I'd imagine she's thinking is, what did I ever do to make him hate me like that?

Sorcha says that Johnny Sarno's on his way up. He wants to shoot the scene where Charles discovers that Trevion's gone, then when he breaks the news to the old dear. She's there, 'We better get you in the bathroom, Fionnuala. Fix up your make-up.'

I turn to go. Erika says that I need to be here for this. I tell her I don't. I really don't. What I need to do is find Ronan and stop myself from focking up Christian's life and probably Ro's as well. I step out into the corridor and try his phone. It's off.

I go back downstairs and make my way back to the roulette table. There's, like, no sign of Ro or Big Juice anywhere. I ring both their rooms, then try Ro's mobile a second time – again, nothing.

It's at that exact point, roysh, that I feel what I immediately know is another trickle of blood coming from my nose. It's the worst bleed I've had yet and I have to put my hand up to my actual face to stop it. Luckily, roysh, there's a gents, like, ten feet away. I walk over to it, push the door and go into Trap One. I pull off maybe twenty sheets of toilet roll and sit on, like, the lid of the jacks with my head back, trying to stop the bleeding. I'm sniffing like a focking madman as well, trying to stop it getting all over my clothes.

It takes, like, ten minutes, roysh, but eventually the bleeding stops. I put the paper in the jacks and flush, then I open the door of the trap . . .

I end up nearly shitting myself there on the spot.

There's, like, three security gords outside the door. And these goys aren't dressed like focking stormtroopers either

– they're the real deal. We're talking nightsticks, we're talking guns, the lot.

One of them sort of, like, throws me out of the way, then rushes into my cubicle and takes a look in the bowl.

'Looks like he flushed it away,' he goes.

I'm there, 'What the fock *is* this?'

'Sir,' he goes, 'we've had a complaint from a member of staff that someone was snorting cocaine in here.'

I catch my reflection in the mirror behind him. There's all, like, dried blood on my upper lip?

I'm there, 'I wasn't snorting anything. I had, like, a nosebleed?'

'Sir,' he goes, except he says it, like, really firmly, 'I'm going to have to ask you to calm down!' the way bouncers do when they're looking for an excuse to deck you.

I'm there, 'But I'm not even into that shit.'

'Let me see some ID,' he goes, like he's not going to take any shit from me.

I hand him my driving licence.

'This you?' he goes.

I'm there, 'Of course it's me.'

'JP Conroy?'

'Yeah.'

One of them sort of, like, grabs my elbow from behind, then another one grabs the other and the third dude goes, 'Sir, we're going to ask you to accompany us to the front of the casino – the police *have* been called.'

I'm like, 'Police? Whoa – you're making, like, a major mistake here.'

They literally pick me up and carry me out of the jacks and I'm suddenly like the coyote out of the *Road Runner* when he goes off the cliff – as in my legs are moving but they're just, like, treading air.

Out of the corner of my eye, I cop C-3PO, over by the craps tables, trying to look all innocent. There's no prizes for guessing who the member of staff was.

I'm there, 'You're a focking grass, 3PO!' except I'm not sure if he hears me, roysh, because I'm moving pretty fast now and all I can see is the blurred faces of the old man and Darth Maul and Sorcha and Erika and Bib Fortuna and Helen and a couple of Gamorrean Gords and Ronan and Big Juice and the old dear in her wedding dress, tears still streaking her face, then finally Christian, Lauren and little Ross, staring at me open-mouthed as I'm carried, like a battering ram, through the gaming hall and the lobby and into the back of a waiting cop cor.

'Fourteen hours!' I'm banging on the cell door, going. 'Fourteen focking hours! Either chorge me or release me.'

I don't know where that line comes from – probably *CSI* or one of those.

The cell's got, like, a bed, a table and two chairs, although the only thing you really need to know about it is that it smells of piss.

The door swings open and a cop walks in. His name's, like, Pat Patterson. I met him earlier and he told me his great-great-grandfather was from Limerick, like this was something to be proud of? I cracked on to be impressed, of course, and told him that Limerick was a beautiful port of the world.

He leans against the wall. 'We picked you up at three this afternoon,' he goes, then makes a big point of looking at his watch. 'It's ten to seven.'

I'm there, 'Yeah? And your point is?'

'My point is, JP, that's not even *four* hours.'

I'm like, 'Facts and figures – whatever. *My* point is, why am I still here? What did the medical examiner say?'

He checked me out just after I got here.

'Quite a bit,' he goes. 'Did you know you've got a septal perforation?'

I'm like, 'Yeah, I'm *kind* of aware of that at this stage? But what did he say about the whole, I don't know, coke thing?'

'Well, from his examination of your pupils, and the swabs he took from your nose, it was, in his opinion, highly unlikely that you ingested any illicit drug in the previous twelve hours.'

'Dude, that's what I told you – my life's a natural high . . .'

He laughs – Pat's actually sound?

'So, like, what am I still doing here?'

'The Federal boys want to talk to you,' he goes.

I'm there, 'The Federal boys? That sounds suspiciously like The Feds to me.'

'That's right.'

'Er, do you mind me asking why?'

I'm suddenly kacking it, thinking they've obviously searched the room and found the laptop and the radio mic.

But it's not that at all.

'It seems there's an arrest warrant outstanding for you since 2001.'

'For me?'

'Yeah, a complaint you slapped a kid around in some toy store in New York?'

My hort nearly stops. Of course, the obvious thing to do is to tell him that I'm not *actually* JP Conroy? But I know one or two goys from Clongowes who did jail time over here for carrying fake ID and it's a generally accepted fact that I'm too pretty to go to prison.

'I'd hordly say *slapped around,*' I go. 'If anything, it was just one good slap?'

'Well, whatever – the kid's coming up here with his parents. Hey, do you have any objection to taking part in a line-up?'

I'm there, 'Er, no.'

He nods. 'Hey, speaking of kids,' he goes, 'yours is here.'

I'm there, 'Ronan? Look, whatever he did, it was my idea,' automatically thinking the worst.

'He didn't do nothing. He came to see you.'

'Oh – well, that's one good thing.'

'Hey, what a great kid . . .'

'Yeah, he definitely has a way with, like, people?'

'The sergeant here – been here forty years. Got some great Mob stories. They're sitting out there for hours talking.'

His voice drops to, like, a whisper. 'Look,' he goes, 'I shouldn't really do this. But like I said, the boys all love him. I'm going to let him in to see you.'

I'm there, 'Really?'

'Hey,' he goes, 'what harm can it do?'

I'm tempted to tell him to frisk him for explosives. Knowing Ro, he's come with an escape plan.

So off he goes and ten or fifteen minutes later, roysh, the cell door swings open again and in walks Ro, looking majorly pissed off with me. 'You're some fooken tulip,' he goes.

I'm there, 'What?'

He looks over his shoulder. 'I feel it only fair to tell you, Rosser, Big Juice is not a happy man.'

I'm there, 'So you didn't go ahead with the whole, I suppose, scam?'

'What, with the heat you drew on us? What do you think?'

He sits down at the table, opposite me, and sighs, I think the word is, *wearily*?

Something suddenly occurs to me. 'Hey, what name did you use when you asked for me?'

'JP Conroy. Don't worry, I'm wide. I remembered you talking to that speed cop and I thought, "I know what this bag of piss is going to do." What are you at, Man? Tell them who you are.'

I'm there, 'No focking way. I could end up getting, like, six months – do you know what they do to pretty boys in the prisons over here? Even best case, I'd be, like, deported? Which'd mean no second series of the show.'

'So, what, you're gonna take the fooken rap for what JP did?'

'Ro, there isn't going to be any rap. I'm just thinking here, they're setting up, like, an ID parade? So they send the kid in. He walks the line. If he doesn't pick me out, they *have* to release me? I'm telling you, I'm going to be back on The Strip in time for the big porty.'

The funny thing, roysh, is that as I'm saying it, I'm storting to relax more? I'm even looking forward to hearing Christian's speech and wondering will I get a mench.

'Take my advice,' Ronan goes, 'tell them the fooken troot.'

I'm like, 'Ro, forget it. Now this scam of yours, is it fixable – as in, could we do it somewhere else?'

He shakes his head. 'I think Big Juice was getting cold feet in anyhow. Ah, we're gonna do something diffordent, even if it's just counting cards?'

'Counting cords? Like Dustin Hoffman?'

He goes, 'You don't have to be autistic, Rosser, to track the ratio of high cards to low cards in a deck and determine the probability advantages . . .'

It's only now, roysh, sitting there in the cop shop, that I suddenly realize how proud I am to hear my son talking like that.

'It's just a matter of assigning a positive, negative or null value to each card in the deck,' he goes, 'then adjusting the running count as each card is dealt. Two to six are plus one. Tens, aces and paints are minus one. Seven, eight, nine are zero . . .'

'Fionn said they think you're gifted,' I go. 'In other words, freakishly intelligent?'

He nods, roysh, like he's taking it all in his stride.

'Don't you worry,' I go, 'I'm not going to let them experiment on you.'

The door suddenly opens. Pat's back. 'You ready for this line-up?' he goes.

I'm there, 'Right with you, Pat.'

Ronan looks me dead in the eye. 'Just fooken tell them, Rosser.'

I actually laugh. 'Ro,' I go. 'Piece of piss.'

So the next thing I know, roysh, I'm in this room with, like, five or six other dudes, who are all around my age? We're actually having a bit of craic because it turns out they're all, like, students and they do this just for the shekels. I stort telling them some of the shit we did for dosh when we were over here on our J1ers and they're cracking their holes laughing – really loving me, if that doesn't come across as, like, too big-headed?

'Hey, aren't you that guy from that show?' one of them goes.

I'm there, 'Er, yeah – but do me a favour, keep it to yourself.'

'Man,' he goes, 'I love that fucking show,' and he high-fives me.

Another cop comes in and tells us to quit talking and to line up against the wall. There's a whole *The Usual Suspects* vibe to it? They've even got the, like, height measures painted on the wall behind us.

'Okay, bring him in,' the cop shouts.

I turn to the dude beside me and tell him they should all come to the casino opening tonight – as in, the new *Star Wars* casino? I happen to be best mates with the dude who project-managed it. He even named his kid after me, if you can believe that. He says that'd be awesome. I tell him I'll be out of here in, like, fifteen minutes.

And then in walks the kid.

I feel my body go instantly cold. I'm thinking, no way. No *focking* way. This has got to be someone's idea of a joke.

He walks the line, roysh, spending a good four or five seconds studying each face. I'm shitting Baileys, of course. Not only am I trying to *not* look like JP, I'm also trying to *not* look like me.

Then I'm thinking, there's a good chance he won't recognize me with the new nose. But I'm sweating like a fat bird writing her first love letter.

He's suddenly standing in front of me, staring hord at my face. I'm doing all sorts of shit, like squinting my eyes and pouting my lips to try to, like, throw him off the trail – but there's obviously something familiar about my face.

It's just he can't place it.

He's just about to move on to the next dude when he suddenly stops and I watch the – I suppose – realization dawn across his face. Our eyes sort of, like, lock, for ten, maybe fifteen seconds, then I watch *his* eyes narrow. He suddenly smiles at me, the little prick.

'Number six,' Danny Lintz goes. 'It's number six.'

Pat Patterson says he's sorry he has to cuff me. I tell him it's cool. He pushes my head down to make sure I don't bang it getting into the back of the cor.

He gets in and storts the engine. He turns on the siren, roysh, but then changes his mind.

The gate rolls upwards and we come up from the underground cor pork. There's, like, a crowd waiting outside. They're mostly, like, reporters, but then I stort picking out one or two familiar faces as well. Sorcha and Erika. Fionn and JP. Christian and Lauren. The old man and Ro. And Honor. All standing by me, no matter what.

There's no sign of the old dear, though, and that sort of, like, winds me like a kick in the stomach.

They're all waving at me. But with my hands cuffed, I

obviously can't wave back. Honor recognizes me even through the glass. 'Daddy!' she's going. 'Daddy!'

Johnny Sarno's loving it, of course. He's got, like, two cameras trained on the cor and two or three more on the crowd. I suppose he's thinking – like we all are – what a focking series finale.

The cor makes its slow way through the crowd, Pat shouting at people through the speaker on the roof, to get out of the way. There's a lot of flashbulbs going off in my boat.

Then, all of a sudden, we're clear of them and I'm looking back through the rear window at the madness, getting smaller and smaller, until it finally disappears and I'm left thinking, so that was it then – that was fame.

I feel suddenly, I don't know, empty, although I do realize I'm getting off lightly here. It took twenty-four hours for me to persuade them that I was Ross O'Carroll-Kelly, not JP Conroy.

The District Attorney wanted to chorge me with all sorts. It turns out his son is, like, a major fan of the show. Two nights ago he called his mother a focking truffle-hunter and I don't need to tell you who they blamed.

'Hey, you're lucky the sergeant took a shine to that kid of yours,' Pat goes.

I laugh. If only they knew.

Soon, we're taking the slipway for McCarron International Airport. Pat suddenly turns up the radio. There's some shit on the news about home repossessions. 'Hey, that's only going to get worse,' he goes. 'You hear Bear Stearns said today they got serious problems with two of their hedge funds?'

I turn around – as anyone would – and I go, 'Er, this affects me *how* exactly?'

Acknowledgements

I would like to, very humbly, thank the wonderful team that continues to support me in my endeavours. Rachel Pierce is more than just an editor to me – she's my director, and a truly great one, too. Rachel, thank you for working so tirelessly, while never allowing the quality to suffer. Thank you, Faith O'Grady – I'm truly blessed to have you as my agent and friend. Thank you, Michael McLoughlin, Patricia Deevy, Cliona Lewis, Patricia McVeigh, Brian Walker and all the Penguin Ireland team – it's a pleasure and a privilege working with you. I'd like to thank my friend Paul O'Kelly for allowing me to pick his enormous brain on the subject of mathematics. Thank you, Alan Clarke, for your quiet-spoken genius. Thanks to my father and my brothers for their love and support and all the fun years. And thank you, Mary, for making me happy.